"Are you and Aunt Lisa going to get married?"

"Why do you ask that?" he said to Rose.

"Because I heard Grandma Sullivan say that it's wrong for you to live together without being married."

Leave it to my mother, Sully thought.

He was at a loss as to how to answer her question, but he knew he had to give it a go.

He was about to say no, when he thought about it.

Married to Lisa?

He could almost imagine being married to her. They laughed together. They had Rose in common, bull riding and the big house on twenty acres. They both liked RV-ing, and chili, and cowboy boots. He grinned. And the sex was great, too.

Some marriages were built on less.

Life *had* been pretty amazing during this arrangement.

So exactly what was his answer to Rose's question?

Dear Reader,

When airline pilot Lisa Phillips and bull rider Brett "Sully" Sullivan become the custodians of their three-year-old niece, their lives immediately change. Lisa has to figure out how she can fly all over the world and still be there when little Rose needs her. And how can Sully be a father when he's driving all over North America in his motor home to ride the Professional Bull Riders circuit? As a top rider who's close to becoming number one in the world, he can't hang up his spurs yet—not at this critical time.

To give Rose some stability and security, Lisa and Sully have to live together in a big Victorian in the upstate New York countryside. Trouble is, they've never even liked each other! Lisa thinks that Sully is just a tumbleweed and a playboy. He thinks Lisa is snobby, stiff and icy. They'll need a miracle to form a family and keep their sense of humor!

As I was writing *Lassoed into Marriage,* I kept thinking how life can change with the blink of an eye. Would I fall apart, or rise to the challenge?

My wish for you is that all of your challenges be light and your rewards great.

I'd love to hear from you. I can be contacted through www.christinewenger.com or at P.O. Box 1823, Cicero, NY, 13039.

Chris Wenger

LASSOED INTO MARRIAGE

CHRISTINE WENGER

HARLEQUIN® SPECIAL EDITION®

Recycling programs
for this product may
not exist in your area.

ISBN-13: 978-0-373-65750-6

LASSOED INTO MARRIAGE

Printed in U.S.A.

Books by Christine Wenger

Harlequin Special Edition

*How to Lasso a Cowboy #2129
*Lassoed into Marriage #2268

Silhouette Special Edition

The Cowboy Way #1662
Not Your Average Cowboy #1788
The Cowboy and the CEO #1846
†It's That Time of Year #1937
†The Tycoon's Perfect Match #1980
*The Cowboy Code #2094

†The Hawkins Legacy
*Gold Buckle Cowboys

CHRISTINE WENGER

has worked in the criminal justice field for more years than she cares to remember. She has a master's degree in probation and parole studies and sociology from Fordham University, but the knowledge gained from such studies certainly has not prepared her for what she loves to do most—write romance! A native central New Yorker, she enjoys watching professional bull riding and rodeo with her favorite cowboy, her husband, Jim.

Chris would love to hear from readers. She can be reached by mail at P.O. Box 1823, Cicero, NY, 13039 or through her website at www.christinewenger.com.

To my very special friends and fans
of the Professional Bull Riders: Pat Prestin of Florida,
Marilyn Day of Illinois and Necia Green of Australia.

And to PBR champion Chris Shivers of Louisiana:
I'll miss watching you ride, but enjoy your retirement!

Chapter One

The door of the huge, white Victorian opened and Brett "Sully" Sullivan walked in, his cowboy boots making a dull thud on the gleaming hardwood floor.

Standing in the middle of the great room, he seemed to be larger than life, larger than the room. He held his black cowboy hat to one side, nervously turning it between his thumb and index finger.

Lisa Phillips hadn't seen Sully in three years, and time had been good to him. His pitch-black hair was cut short with haphazard peaks on the top, and it gave him a devil-may-care look that fit his personality. Without the boots and hat and in his gray suit and maroon tie, he looked more like a lawyer than the bull rider that he was.

"Where's Rose?" Sully asked, his turquoise-blue eyes full of concern.

"She's in her room. My parents and your parents are

putting her to bed," Lisa answered, spooning sugar into her coffee.

He nodded then shifted on his feet. He seemed not to know whether to stay or go. He probably wanted to retreat back into his motor home instead of trying to make polite conversation with neighbors and relatives who were paying their respects.

Lisa would just like to fly to some place tropical. Some place where she could soak up the rays and water on a beach…and maybe stop crying.

"Is that coffee?" Sully finally asked.

"Yes. And it's hot and strong."

He pulled out a chair next to her and helped himself from the pot that someone had graciously put in front of her on a silver tray. She noticed that he drank his black—just like a tough cowboy should.

Lisa thought back to the day of Rose's christening. She and Sully were Rose's godparents and it had been a festive affair. No, it was a festive weekend—in direct contrast to today.

The evening of the christening, Rick and Carol, Sully's brother and her sister, had called a meeting with the two of them and asked them to be Rose's guardians in case something happened to them.

Lisa was stunned yet flattered that she had been chosen to see to Rose's upbringing.

Then the unthinkable happened.

Rick and Carol were gone now. Deceased. Their car had hydroplaned during a rainstorm and hit a bridge support. Rose was with them in the car, but she escaped without a scratch, safely belted into her car seat.

The realization that she'd never see her sister, Carol, again rocked her from her hair roots to her toes, and tears pooled in her eyes. When would she ever stop crying?

And Rose… She was an orphan now.

And she and Sully were Rose's guardians.

"Sully?"

"Yeah?"

He turned to her. His blue eyes were red-rimmed and bloodshot. For a second, she felt sorry for the cowboy. Rick was his brother and her brother-in-law. She had loved Rick, too.

"Remember sitting here three years ago?" she asked. "Rick and Carol had us sign guardianship papers."

"Yeah."

"We're Rose's guardians now."

"I know." He pushed his cowboy hat back with a thumb. "I never thought in a million years that—"

"Me, either. I'm not cut out to be a mother."

"I'll be the worst father in the world."

"What was my sister thinking?"

"My brother must have been drunk."

Lisa took a sip of coffee. It was too strong, so she added more cream. "What do we do now?"

"Damned if I know."

Lisa kicked off her heels and shrugged out of her black blazer that matched her black skirt. Sighing, she thought how she hated the suit, which she reserved for funerals.

In the mirror on the wall she noticed that her pale blond hair had frizzed in the drizzling rain at the cemetery. Her face looked drained of all color despite the makeup she'd applied.

She was trying to hold her emotions together, but she felt another wave of tears threatening. All she wanted to do was to find the nearest bedroom, pull the comforter over her head and sleep. When she woke, she'd find that all of this had just been a nightmare.

Before they could talk anymore, the doorbell rang and

more neighbors arrived, carrying casseroles and cakes. Lisa let the capable Mrs. Turner from across the street handle everything, bless her.

As if someone had turned up the volume on a TV talk show, the high-ceilinged room came alive with noise. Both sets of their parents, Gordon and Betsy Sullivan and Clyde and Melanie Phillips, were deep in discussion. It soon reached a crescendo.

"We can take the child," Betsy said. "We have more than enough room at our Palm Beach condo. Eighth floor. Great views."

"You can't raise Rose in a condo," Melanie argued. "We live in a child-friendly commune in Kentucky. She'll have a lot of children to play with."

"And to dig a new outhouse with at your commune," Gordon added.

"How dare you!" Melanie pointed a finger at him. Former army colonel or not, she wasn't going to tolerate that kind of slam against her parents from Sully's father.

Sully stood up from the table, oozing authority. "That's enough," he said firmly.

Lisa nodded. "I don't want Rose to hear her grandparents snapping at one another. Rose's guardians have already been decided, and Sully and I are them!"

"I don't want any fighting," Sully said. "And I'm sure that you already know about Carol and Rick's wishes."

A deep voice cut through the noise. "I'm sure that they know, too."

Everyone turned in the direction of a distinguished white-haired man in a three-piece suit.

"I'm Carol and Rick's lawyer, Glen Randolph. I'm so sorry to interrupt, but my clients, who were also my good friends, warned me that this would happen. So while everyone is still here, I'd like to meet with Rose's grandparents and Brett and Lisa." The lawyer looked around at the guests who had stopped their conversations to listen. "Let's adjourn to Rick's office."

The capable Mrs. Turner waved them away and called for the remaining guests to help themselves at the buffet table.

Little Rose's relatives followed the lawyer soundlessly, single file.

After they all took a seat, they looked at him expectedly.

"Like I said, I'm Glen Randolph, and I was a personal friend of Carol and Rick." He paused, making eye contact with each of them. He opened an accordion folder and pulled out a handful of typed papers. "As you know, they named Brett and Lisa as Rose's guardians, and—"

"Sully? Are you aware that my son lives in a motor home?" Gordon Sullivan interrupted. "He's a shiftless bull rider, for heaven's sake. He travels from one bull riding event to the next. What can he offer a three-year-old?"

Gordon's face was red, and Lisa thought he was going to have a heart attack. Although she wasn't a Sully fan, she didn't particularly like what Gordon was saying about him.

Oh, all right, she might as well admit that she thought the same thing about Sully.

Sully bit down on his lower lip. "Rick trusted me with his daughter. I won't let him down."

"And I won't let Carol down," Lisa added.

"How can you say that?" Her mother rolled her eyes. "You're just like Sully, Lisa. You can't stay in one place long enough to raise a child. You fly those diesel-guzzling biohazard planes all over creation. You pay good money for an apartment that you're never at. How do you expect to raise a three-year-old?"

I'm just like Sully?

No way!

"You two are going to make quite the couple," her father said.

"We're not a couple," Lisa stated.

"That's for sure," Sully added under his breath.

Sully tapped his fingers on Rick's desk. His large turquoise ring bobbed up and down. This was the same ring he had been wearing three years ago at Rose's christening. Lisa remembered it. Funny, she remembered a lot of things about him.

And even though she didn't care a fig about him, for some reason she looked for him on TV when the Professional Bull Riders events were on. He was riding hot lately and was near the top in the standings.

He couldn't ride and take care of Rose at the same time.

She couldn't fly and take care of Rose at the same time.

Lisa swallowed hard. She needed an income. She needed to fly. She was a pilot. That's what she did. That's what she was.

The lawyer continued, "I will be making surprise visits to ensure Rose is thriving under their care. This is as per the instructions of Carol and Rick. They have also left a generous stipend for the care of Rose, which I'll dispense monthly for her needs. Carol and Rick also requested that Rose be raised in this house and have left it to Lisa and Brett. It's paid in full. There is also a trust fund for Rose for when she either goes to college or turns twenty-one. They have also left a personal note for Lisa and Brett."

Mr. Randolph handed the letter to Lisa. "You might want to read it at a later date."

"Thank you," Lisa mumbled, looking at her name and Sully's written on the envelope in Carol's rolling script. Tears stung her eyes. She'd never be able to pick up the phone and talk to Carol again or hop a plane and visit whenever she needed a vacation or a "Rose fix."

"I know that this is probably overwhelming at this sad time," Mr. Randolph said. "But if Lisa and Sully decide that they cannot accept guardianship, or if they fail my evaluation, then Rose will be awarded to the grandparents. Six months with one pair, and then six months with the other."

The grandparents perked up, but Lisa was appalled. She had forgotten about the six-month split! That wasn't the answer, either. It would be too hard on Rose, too disruptive. Certainly everyone could see that!

Everyone except the grandparents. No doubt they were already mentally packing Rose's bags, certain that she and Sully would fail.

"Any questions?" Mr. Randolph asked.

"I'm asking the grandparents for their cooperation," Sully said. "Lisa, Rose and I need some time to get to know each other. We need time to adjust. So I'm asking that you all leave within a week's time. Feel free to call Rose anytime you'd like." He stood. "Anything you want to add, Lisa?"

"I think that's a perfect plan," she said.

"I'm hoping that you two succeed," her father said. "But we'll be ready anytime you need us. Just call."

Sully's mother fussed with one of her diamond studs. "I'll get Rose's bedroom ready at our condo. Just in case."

"Please, no more remarks like that," Lisa said, standing. "You must know that we'll do our best to raise Rose."

Sully's mother nodded. "You are absolutely right, Lisa. I apologize."

"Thank you," Lisa said, relaxing a little. "I know that you all have Rose's best interest at heart."

Lisa held the precious letter in her hand. Now that the sun was shining, she decided that she'd like to read it in Carol's beautiful garden in the backyard, where the spring flowers were blooming.

Carol always had a green thumb and had spent hours digging in the dirt.

Lisa would much rather skim the clouds in a jet than garden.

"I think we're done here," Mr. Randolph said. "I'll let you get back to your guests."

Lisa made her way through the crowd of people gathered in the house. Mrs. Turner and some helpers were busy refilling the buffet and picking up the discarded paper plates and plastic forks.

As she walked by the gathering around the buffet table, Lisa pasted on a smile, thanking people for coming and for paying their respects. They were a friendly crowd, and Lisa had a pang of regret that she hadn't made friends with any of her own neighbors in Atlanta, but it was near impossible considering her lifestyle.

She made her way out to the backyard to the garden. Sitting down on a concrete bench, she smiled at the little purple resin door in the tulip garden that said, "Carol's Garden. Fairies enter here."

Taking a deep breath, she inhaled the mix of floral scents—daffodils, tulips and hyacinths. That was the part of living in the city that she missed most—the spring flowers that bloomed after the snow. Soon the bulbs would die out and the perennials would bloom, and Carol's garden would be a riot of color and different scents.

Could she possibly keep up Carol's garden? She didn't know a weed from a potential flower.

Could she be a good mother to Rose? She didn't know that, either.

She stared at the back of the huge Victorian, admiring the turrets and the porches that jutted out. It had more rooms than most B&Bs, and she knew that Carol and Rick had wanted more children to fill those rooms.

Looking to her right, she saw a big statue of some goddess—maybe Athena, maybe not. Lisa didn't know her goddesses, but this one was emptying water from some kind of pitcher into a concrete pool.

Currently, Sully was roping Athena. He twirled a rope over his head, then he'd let it loose and it would fly, catching under Athena's breasts and above the pitcher. Every now and then, he'd stop and stare off into the distance, as if he were thinking.

He roped over and over again and stared, until finally he shook his head and walked over to where she was sitting.

"Mind if I sit down?" he asked, loosening his tie and undoing the first few buttons of his shirt. He tossed the rope on the ground.

"Are you done roping?" she asked.

"I always rope when I think."

She moved over to give him room on the bench. "I've been thinking, too."

"We have some decisions to make," he said.

"No kidding. Maybe I should learn to rope, too, so I can sort things out."

Sully raised a perfect black eyebrow. "I'll teach you. It's good therapy."

Why did he have to have eyelashes like paintbrushes? In contrast, she was pale and had to glob on mascara and eyebrow pencil to show that she even had lashes and brows.

His blue eyes met her dark green ones. "First of all, do you think we can work together? I mean, we don't even like each other. Rose will sense that."

He certainly believed in laying his cards on the table, didn't he?

Taking a deep breath, he continued. "We are two adults. And we both love Rose. And there's no way I want her raised by my parents. They're too controlling, especially my father. He always treated Rick and me like army privates. I can't see him with a little girl."

"I don't want her raised by mine, either. They're not controlling enough," Lisa said. "And we don't want her in a foster home with strangers. So we're all she's got."

"Poor kid." Sully smiled, and his eyes twinkled.

Lisa could understand why the buckle bunnies fell at his feet. The cowboy could be charming when he wanted to be.

"Yeah, poor kid," she agreed.

They shared a smile, and Lisa couldn't believe how much they'd agreed on in one sitting, unlike their past history.

Suddenly, Lisa's smile faded and tears cascaded down her cheeks—not for herself, but for Carol and Rick, who'd never see their little girl grow up. And for Rose, of course, who'd never know her parents.

Sully hesitantly reached for her hand, and she didn't have the strength to move it away. She appreciated the gesture. When his hand closed over hers, she could feel his strength, his warmth. For a brief moment, she felt confident that they'd do okay.

"I really don't want her to have to do a six-month split between her grandparents," he said again. "It'd be too disruptive on top of everything."

"I agree, Sully. No way."

"So we're going to have to make this work, Lisa."

"I know. And I'm scared."

"I'm not scared of a crazy, two-thousand-pound bull with horns the size of baseball bats, but I'm damn scared of raising a little girl."

"I've seen Rose with you. You're great with her. And she adores you." All her negative feelings about him aside, it was the truth.

"Back atcha." He shook his head. "But I'm not the kind of guy who can stay in one place for any length of time."

"Neither am I," Lisa said. "And we can't live in your motor home, and my apartment in Atlanta wouldn't work. Carol and Rick wanted Rose raised in this house."

"I know. Rose needs—" He gestured to the huge house. "This white elephant."

"How are we going to earn a living?" Lisa asked. "I know that we have some money coming in from Carol and Rick, but that's Rose's money."

"We're going to have to work something out. I'm really close to winning the Finals this year in Vegas. I need to compete."

Vegas? That was the other side of the country from New York.

"But it's only April, and the PBR Finals are in November," she said, remembering the announcements on TV when she'd watched him ride.

"How do you know that?" he asked. "Do you watch me?"

"Of course not!" she lied. "I must have seen the Finals advertised somewhere."

For some reason, she actually looked forward to the weekend when the bull riding, and Sully, would be on TV. If she was flying, she taped it, and she would never admit that she screamed for him to ride his bull for eight seconds.

Why? She didn't know. On one occasion, it crossed her mind that she might be secretly attracted to Sully, but she quickly dismissed that. She just liked the sport. It was... different. Sully was a minor celebrity who she knew, and he was just someone to cheer for.

"We can worry about Las Vegas later," Lisa said.

"No, we can't. I have to compete to stay high in the rankings to have a chance at winning in Vegas. I have to work the circuit," he said, his right leg bouncing like a nervous tick. "And that means traveling to all the events. By my calculations, there are seventeen left. That's about four a month, with the summer off."

"And I'm going to have to fly, Sully. I need to fly."

He tightened the grip on her hand. "Shall we tell the lawyer that we're not ready yet?" He looked at her with those damn blue eyes.

"That might be the truth, but we can't do that," she said. "And somehow I think Mr. Randolph knows that we don't have the lifestyle to be parents. He's going to be making surprise visits."

"I know."

Lisa sighed. "But besides our jobs, you never liked me, and I never liked you. You are a party animal, and—"

"And you're a drag," he finished.

She raised an eyebrow. "If you're referring to Rose's christening when you got a keg and you persuaded all the men to watch football, play cards and smoke cigars, then, yes, I'm a bore."

"And you certainly speak your mind," he added.

"I certainly do, especially when someone acts like a jerk. Let me remind you about Rick's bachelor party," she said.

"Please don't. I still haven't recovered yet—"

"And then there's the time—"

"When you were such a snob, and—" Sully suddenly stopped. "This isn't the time or the place, Lisa."

"I know."

They sat in silence for a while, until Lisa held up the envelope with the letter her sister and Rick had written. "You know, other than our parents, we were Carol and Rick's only alternative. We're their only siblings. At least on my side, we don't have any close relatives."

"My side, either," Sully said.

"See? They had no other choice. Still, I can't bring myself to open the letter yet."

She tried to hand the envelope to him, but he held his hands up like a traffic cop.

"You'll open it when you're ready," he said. "Then we'll read it together."

How did cowboy get so smart?

"We love Rose." He met her gaze, and for a nanosecond, she got lost in the depths of his eyes. "And that's why we can put our differences aside and do this."

Lisa looked down and thought.

We're just too different, but as long as Sully's willing to try, so am I.

Chapter Two

"I want my mommy and daddy," Rose said, tears swimming in her eyes. "I don't want them to be in heaven. I want them right here."

The pure-white cat, Snowball, who was curled up beside Rose, stared at the little girl's face. Molly, a small, black, short-haired mutt, looked at her from the floor.

Lisa smiled. She'd never had pets growing up, but Snowball and Molly must have sensed Rose's duress. They hadn't left the little girl's side for very long since her parents had died.

Lisa sat on the sofa, on the other side of Rose, her arms around the girl's slight shoulders. Grandparents Sullivan and Phillips had all left for the airport this morning, and the house was blissfully silent.

Lisa had been reading Rose a book, and things were going well until Rose closed the book, her bottom lip quivering. "I don't want them to be in heaven."

"Your mommy and daddy are thinking of you all the time, just like you think of them," Lisa said, hugging her niece closer to her.

She wished she could think of something more soothing to say to Rose, but she missed her sister so very much. She couldn't even think about never talking to her again, never hearing her laugh. She wished her faith was strong enough for her to believe that someday they'd see each other again—somehow.

"They're watching you from heaven, sweetie, and they love you very much. Just like I love you and Uncle Sully loves you. And don't forget all your grandparents. They love you, too."

She wiped Rose's tears with a tissue and had her blow her nose. Molly rested her chin on Rose's leg, and Rose reached down to pet the dog, then opened the book and started turning the pages, pointing to objects in the pictures and identifying them.

Lisa let her mind wander. It was hard to believe that a week had gone by since she and Sully had moved into Carol and Rick's house. She hoped that someday the big Victorian would feel like her own home—well, hers and Sully's and Rose's.

Because she hadn't gone back to Atlanta yet to get all her clothes, she'd been doing countless loads of laundry from what she'd brought in her suitcase. It had crossed her mind that she could borrow a couple of Carol's tees and maybe a pair of shorts until she could go shopping, but she just couldn't do it, couldn't go into the master bedroom.

So she'd closed the door.

Sully had moved some of his clothes into a bedroom opposite hers on the first floor, but Lisa knew that he often sneaked out at night and wandered—out to his motor home, out on the front porch or the back porch, back in again. It was impossible not to hear him open the creaky doors and his boots clunk on the wooden floor as she lay awake nights, not able to sleep.

"Why don't you read to me, Rose? You know the story."

Rose wiped her nose on her sleeve and moved the book to her lap. Lisa smiled as her niece made up a story of a bunny going to the market and buying vegetables for a party he was having with his other woodland friends.

But Lisa barely heard Rose, thinking instead of how she should have gone to the grocery store or sent Sully and Rose with a list.

Sully didn't mind doing errands. Matter of fact, he and Rose had a routine that he called their "walk around." They'd drive to the village of Salmon Falls, park the van and have breakfast at Salmon Falls Diner. Rose would have cereal with a banana or, if she felt adventurous, she'd have a pancake.

Then it'd be off to the drugstore, the post office, the grocery store—wherever she'd sent them on errands—and they'd stop at the playground on the Village Square, where Rose would play. Sully called it her "swing and sing" time because she would make up songs and sing them as she swung.

She wondered who looked forward to their walk arounds more, Sully or Rose.

The walk arounds had started when the grandparents had become overwhelming, which was their second day here. Sully had pulled Lisa aside and told her that Rose needed a break from their constant hovering and trying to outdo one another. He said that he'd take Rose out to run errands for her.

That was considerate of him, but Lisa had wanted to come, too. They weren't the only ones who needed a break from the grandparents.

She was always the responsible one; Sully was the fun guy. But as they raised Rose, she didn't want to be cast into the role of disciplinarian while Sully was the one she had a good time with.

Based on the previous week, Rick and Carol were right in not picking a set of grandparents as guardians for Rose. She and Sully might not be the best prize behind curtain number one, but they couldn't be any worse than the Sullivans or the Phillipses.

She could hear the drone of the bright-green lawn mower as it made its rounds in the front yard. After enough hints from her, Sully had finally stopped roping the darn statue and got the ride-on mower out of the shed.

After tinkering for hours and taking numerous coffee breaks, he'd finally got it working.

As she and Rose heard the mower approach, they both turned around on the sofa to look out the big picture window at Sully. Lisa kneeled next to Rose, who stood, and they waved to him.

In response, Sully raised an arm into the air. They heard him yell "Yee-haw" as he went by. On his next pass, he did the same thing. On the way back, he took off his cowboy hat and was fanning the engine.

He stopped the lawn mower, making like he was getting off a bull. Then he bowed to his audience.

He got back on, pushed the lever and clearly expected the mower to go forward, but it went in reverse.

The surprise on his face was priceless.

She and Rose laughed at him, and he feigned anger. They laughed even harder.

They'd both needed it.

Sully was good for Rose.

Maybe he was good for her, too.

Rose was occupied watching Sully, so Lisa went into the

laundry room to put in yet another load of her clothes and Rose's. Sully did his own laundry.

So far, they were doing okay, but the real test would come now—when it was just the three of them.

After loading the washer, she went into Rick's office and turned to a website that she'd flagged—a basic website for young cooks. What the mothers had had her cooking was way too complicated. Probably that's what they were counting on to use as ammunition for Mr. Randolph.

She'd have to look for something really easy and nutritious for Rose to eat. And Sully. She supposed that he'd eat with them, too. Like a family.

And she hoped that whatever she'd make would be eatable and that she wouldn't make them sick.

She could boil water and make pasta with a jar of sauce and pre-made meatballs from the store and she could microwave anything and everything, but they couldn't live on pasta alone.

Even though she could fly jumbo jets, she didn't have a clue how to cook a real meal.

Sully washed his greasy and grass-stained hands at the laundry room sink. The air in the house smelled like something was…burning.

He ran into the kitchen just as the smoke alarm went off. Rose started to cry. The dog started to bark, then whine, and the cat scooted under the living room sofa. Lisa stood in front of the stove, fanning the billowing smoke with a dish towel.

Grabbing two pot holders, he hipped Lisa aside and pulled out a shallow pan with charred lumps of something inside. The pan and the lumps were on fire.

He dumped it, pan and all, into the kitchen sink, not realizing that the sink was full of soapy water. Everything hit the water with a sizzle and a blast of smoke. Then all became silent, even Rose and the dog.

Sully's stomach growled. He hoped that the burned lumps weren't steak. He'd had a hankering for steak.

Lisa's face was as white as the lily on the kitchen table and she wasn't blinking.

"Lisa, are you okay? Did you get burned?" He took her hands and looked them over.

She just stared at him in shock.

"Lisa?" He pulled her to the other half of the sink, the half that didn't contain…uh…dinner. He ran cold water over her hands, still inspecting them for burns or blisters. They looked fine.

Rose had a grip on Lisa's pant leg. Sully winked at her. "Everything's okay, Rose. Lisa's okay. Right, Lisa?"

Eventually, color returned to Lisa's face and lips. He handed her a towel.

"I'm fine, honey. Don't worry," Lisa said, smoothing Rose's hair.

Lisa dried her hands and shook her head. "That was supposed to be ketchup-covered meatloaf, sliced potatoes with oregano and baked carrots. Now it's soapy wet charcoal."

"Don't worry about it." He held out his hand to Rose, and she took it. "Why don't we go out to eat? Where should we go?"

"Pete's Pizza and Polar," Rose answered.

He raised an eyebrow. "Polar?"

"Ice cream," Lisa answered. "We ate there on my last visit." Turning to Rose, she added, "Great idea."

The girl grinned.

"I'm going to jump in the shower. Then I'll be right with you," Sully said.

"And we'll get ready, too," Lisa said, opening the windows over the sink. "It'll be good to get out of here for a while, let the smoke clear."

Sully hurried to his bedroom in the front-left corner of the house and found a clean change of clothes. Then he jumped into the shower off his bedroom.

He shaved in the shower to save a step, cut the water and towel-dried himself off. Slapping on some aftershave, he padded naked into his room and then stopped suddenly, his gaze settling on the closed door. He took a grateful breath, glad that he'd had enough sense to close the door to his bedroom. Alone, in his motor home, he never paid any attention to that kind of thing. However, here in Rick and Carol's house, he had to be more careful.

Rick and Carol's house.

He supposed he should get used to thinking of it as their house, the three of them, but that seemed impossible yet. Maybe being comfortable here would come in due time. And maybe not.

Running a comb through his hair, he made a mental note to stop at a barbershop on his next walk around with Rose. He didn't want to take any ribbing from the TV announcers when they got a gander at his longish hair. They loved making comments about hair and tattoos, feeling that all cowboys must fit a certain mold.

A shot of adrenaline coursed through him whenever he thought of riding bulls. The next event on the circuit would be in Fort Lauderdale, Florida, and it was scheduled this coming Saturday.

Just six days away.

He had to go. If he wanted to keep up his ranking, he had to compete.

Then he had to win the Finals.

Then he would retire.

This chain of events would shore up his career plan to

be a TV announcer for the PBR events. He wanted to do special interviews with the riders and the stock contractors along with the sports medicine doctors, wives and fiancées and whoever else would be of interest to the fans.

He was approaching thirty, and bull riding was a sport for the young. Because he couldn't picture his life without the PBR, announcing and commentating was the next best thing to riding.

He had to win the Finals and win the season to be seriously considered.

From Salmon Falls, Fort Lauderdale would be a twenty-four-hour, nonstop ride in his motor home. He could leave Thursday and be back here by Tuesday morning.

That's just what he'd do.

He grabbed his hat from the top of the dresser and plunked it on his head. As he caught his reflection in the mirror, he realized that something was wrong with his plan.

Lisa and Rose. He had to think of them now.

That was a new twist for him. He had never had to think of anyone else before.

He'd enjoyed his first day alone with Lisa and Rose. He'd spent most of the morning trying to get the mower started and the rest of the day mowing the lawn, so it wasn't much of a test. But so far, so good, in spite of the kitchen disaster.

This arrangement was going to be a snap.

He had to admit that he looked forward to seeing Lisa and Rose every day, and he just loved his outings with Rose. All the shop owners knew her by name, and she knew their names. The regulars at the Salmon Falls Diner looked forward to seeing her every morning, and she glowed from all the attention.

Rose was no shrinking violet.

Sully opened the door, grabbed the keys to Rick's van off the dresser and went to find his two dinner dates.

An hour later, Sully was eating the best pizza he'd ever had. Rose was covered in it, and Lisa was dabbing at the girl's face with a wet tissue.

"Can I play over there?" Rose asked sweetly, pointing. She looked enviously at the children playing in a ball pit inside a bright blue inflated castle.

Lisa looked over at the children yelling and laughing and hesitated. Turning to Sully, she said, "I'm afraid she'll get hurt."

"She'll be fine," he said. "What do you want to do? Go in there with her? Let the kid have some fun!"

"There's a weight limit." Lisa pointed to the sign by the mesh door of the inflatable. "I don't think either of us would qualify."

"I see you've thought of doing just that." Sully chuckled. "There's a worker stationed by the door watching the kids, and we can see Rose from here. Let her go."

"I don't think so," she said.

"Lisa, let it go."

Lisa nodded, then turned to Rose. "Be careful, sweetie."

"I will."

She scampered off, and Sully knew that it was a perfect time to talk to Lisa.

"I have to ride at the event in Fort Lauderdale this weekend," he said, turning to catch a glimpse of Rose in the ball pit.

"She's over there," Lisa pointed, answering his unasked question. Lisa put down her slice of pizza and waved to Rose.

"Lisa, I have to go to Fort Lauderdale."

Lisa dabbed at her mouth with her napkin. "When would you fly out? Saturday? And you'd return on Sunday night?"

"I don't fly. No way. In order for me to get on a plane,

I'd have to be drunk and hog-tied. I like my boots on the ground." He gave a thumbs-up to Rose.

Rose shouted, "Look at me jump, Aunt Lisa!" Rose did a belly flop into the bright balls. Lisa clapped and the little girl grinned.

When Rose turned to talk to a newly found friend, Lisa asked Sully, "Why don't you fly, Mr. Adrenaline Rush Bull Rider?"

"I keep thinking of Newton's law of gravity. Like, how do three or four tons of metal, glass and luggage take off and stay up in the sky?" Sully waved when he saw Rose looking at them.

"Do you want the technical answer to that?" Lisa asked.

"I wouldn't believe you anyway." He grinned. "That's why I bought a motor home—so I can drive to events. I plan on leaving Thursday for Fort Lauderdale, and I'll be back on Tuesday."

"Are you asking me or telling me, Sully?" She clapped as Rose did a belly flop into the balls.

"I'm not used to asking anyone for permission, so I guess I'm telling you." He laughed as Rose scrambled to stand and didn't quite make it.

Lisa crossed her arms in front of her chest and sat back in her chair, looking at Sully for the first time since they'd started talking. "We knew this day would come, didn't we?"

He nodded. "I'll go to Florida, and in exchange I'll let you fly somewhere."

Lisa turned back to Rose. "You'll *let* me fly? Let me?"

Sully shook his head. This wasn't going right at all. "Did I put my boot in my mouth?"

"Try both boots."

Sully pushed his hat back with a thumb. Most of the time Lisa reminded him of his second grade teacher, Mrs. Moth.

The only thing she was missing was a ruler ready to crash down on his knuckles.

"You know what I'm trying to say, Lisa," he said.

"Let me backtrack a moment, please." She cleared her throat. "You stuck me with both sets of parents while you disappeared with Rose for most of the day every day of their visit. The rest of the time you hid in your motor home. I'm going stir-crazy."

"Sorry about the stir-crazy part." He nodded. "And you're absolutely right. Sorry about abandoning you, but our mothers insisted on teaching you how to cook."

"And both of our fathers enjoyed the spectacle," she snapped.

He supposed he had unconsciously—or maybe consciously—stuck her with them all, but he'd had to get out of there. He was used to peace and quiet and solitude, for the most part.

When he was parked at one of the arenas and wanted company, all he had to do was walk out the door of his RV. Most of the other bull riders were there in their motor homes or truck campers, too. They'd all pitch in for potluck meals, and most of the time they'd all sit out in lawn chairs and talk until it was time to get ready for the event. Sometimes, it was like one big tailgate party and he could jump right into that. But most of the time, it was quiet.

A loud squeal came from the direction of the ball pit and both of them stood, searching for Rose. She was rolling around in the colorful balls, and Sully wished that he'd brought his camera.

"So, I'd like a change of scenery and want to get out of the house for a while," Lisa said. "Here's the deal. You can go to the bull riding on two conditions." She sat back down.

He met her gaze. This was even worse than second grade

at Mountain View Grammar School with Mrs. Moth. He slowly sat down.

"I'm listening," he said, dreading her conditions already. She held up two fingers, just like Mrs. Moth. "One, I get two flights with you taking care of Rose."

"Agreed." That was easy.

"And two, Rose and I go with you to Fort Lauderdale."

He pointed to his chest. "Didn't I just rant about how I don't fly?"

"We'd all go in your motor home. And we'll make it a week-long trip. It would be the perfect opportunity for all of us to get to know one another—to bond, so to speak."

He fished for the words, and with his mouth flapping, he probably looked like a freshly caught trout. Rose would love the trip, but he wondered how he and Lisa would get along in such cramped quarters.

"Us? Together for a week in my small motor home? Wouldn't you and I kill each other?" he asked.

"Perhaps." Lisa laughed, and he liked when she did that. As far as he was concerned, she didn't laugh enough, but he wouldn't count that against her just yet. She'd just lost her sister. Still, on the handful of occasions when they'd met in the past, she seemed to sit in judgment of him—and she appeared to find him lacking.

Granted, most of those occasions were party times—Rick's bachelor's party, the Super Bowl, Rick and Carol's wedding, Rose's christening—and he loved to party. Still, she didn't have to seem so prim and proper all the time.

Did she ever have fun?

"Uncle Sully, Aunt Lisa, look at me!" Rose shouted.

They both looked as their niece jumped into the balls for the hundredth time. Lisa clapped and Sully whistled loudly and shrilly as if he were calling a bull for dinner.

"Sully." Lisa inhaled deeply, and he braced himself for

what she was going to say. "I think I'm going to put my name on the list for private charters for now instead of working a regular schedule with Cardinal Global. Private charters are on an as-needed basis, and JFW Aviation flies out of Albany, so that's convenient to Salmon Falls and totally doable."

He breathed a little easier. "Sounds like a good idea."

"That's what I was thinking. It'll work out better for Rose."

"I really appreciate that, Lisa. I do." It was a totally nice and unexpected concession on her part. He'd do his best to reciprocate.

She nodded. "So, what about my idea of all of us traveling together to Fort Lauderdale?"

He paused, his hands itching for his rope and the cement statue so he could weigh the pros and cons more thoroughly. "Let's do it," he blurted.

Lisa held out her hand, and they shook. As his rough and calloused hand closed around hers, he decided that he liked her style. Keep everything businesslike, negotiable, but do the best they could do for Rose.

He looked over yet again at Rose jumping on the balls, her face red with laughter, her hair wet from the exertion. She was having a great time, and maybe for a while, she'd forget that she'd lost her mommy and daddy.

In their place were Aunt Lisa and Uncle Sully—pale substitutes for her parents.

He knew that he and Lisa would do their best to raise Rose. Yes, he made a slight blunder not asking Lisa if he could ride at the Fort Lauderdale event, but for heaven's sake, he wasn't a kid having to ask a parent for permission.

Well, okay, okay. Maybe he had to stop thinking of just himself. And, yeah, once in a while he could ask Lisa to go on his walk arounds with Rose. She'd dropped enough hints.

But sometimes he had to get away from her, too. Sometimes she could be just as demanding and rigid as his parents.

Especially when she looked at him with her green eyes flashing disappointment.

He'd never have a nine-to-five job. He'd always be ready for a party or to throw one of his own. He'd make sure that Rose would have a fun, happy life. Lisa could take care of the blah, boring stuff.

Sully knew he'd never measure up to Lisa's expectations, nor did he want to even try.

So, he was going to hit the trail with his new family, and he'd try to get along with Mrs. Moth…er…Lisa Phillips.

Chapter Three

Three days later, Sully drove his rig back from downtown Salmon Falls. He loved the little town, loved the sidewalks, the flowers, the town square. He loved that there were no chain stores or chain eateries, and how the little shops were just that...little.

He'd just left Marv's Garage. Marv was the town's hangout for gearheads, gossip central for men and the home to a bottomless coffeepot.

Though Sully had gone over his motor home from top to bottom, he'd figured that Marv should check it anyway.

Marv had cleared the RV and everything was ready to rock.

When he pulled up in front of the Victorian, Lisa and Rose were ready to pack the RV. Over the next hour they made several trips to the vehicle, carrying loads of clothes, food, toys, shoes and more shoes. Heaven only knew what they'd put in the small bathroom cupboard. And there were plastic containers stacked all over containing bottles and tubes of stuff.

Lisa and Rose had gone shopping, so the closets and cabinets were overflowing with their purchases. That was okay with him. He traveled light. Mostly, whatever he needed—his wrap tape, rosin, bull rope and bell, jeans, shirts, underwear, socks and a couple of riding gloves—was in his gear bag.

Last night, he'd slipped out of his room in the Victorian and sat at the kitchen table with a map of the East Coast. He plotted the route he wanted to take and flagged some campgrounds along the way. Remembering how Rick had told him that Rose loved the water, he flagged the ones with swimming areas for her. He'd programmed them into his GPS.

Lisa and Rose were back with Molly and Snowball and yet more plastic containers. Sully looked on in amazement.

"Hey, we can't fit the whole house into this motor home, ladies. We're camping, not moving into a mansion in Beverly Hills."

Lisa chuckled. "This is the last load—well, except for more food."

"We bought hot dogs. And stuff for sloppy joe's," Rose announced to him. "And beans in a can…for you. Aunt Lisa said that cowboys like beans."

Sully looked at Lisa. "Beans, huh?" He winked at Rose. "Well, your aunt was right. I do like beans…in a can."

As a matter of fact, they'd already loaded in a supply of microwaveable foods—beans, hot dogs, chicken and TV dinners.

Since the burned meatloaf incident, Lisa had given the oven in the house a wide berth, like it was a Brahma ready to charge at her, but the microwave was her pet.

He had both in the motor home.

Rose looked up at him with brown eyes, the color of his brother Rick's. "When are we going to see Mickey Mouse?"

Huh? There wouldn't be any time for that! He raised an eyebrow at Lisa. "We'll leave as soon as Aunt Lisa is ready."

"I just need to lock up the house, and that's it," she said. Her face was flushed, maybe from slogging everything, but Sully liked to think that she was excited to go on the trip.

That would be a change for her—being excited about something.

She dropped an armload of groceries on the table. "You could have helped, you know."

"I was securing everything," he said. "Can't have all those plastic boxes flying around."

"I'll do it. I'll do everything." She rolled her eyes, turned and left the RV.

What was her problem?

He shrugged it off, hoping that everything would go well on this trip. If it did, maybe he could convince her to travel to the next stop on the bull riding circuit.

He'd have to get through this trip to Florida first.

Lisa didn't seem to be the camping type, although traveling in a motor home was a step up from camping. He thought of camping as backpacking or pitching a tent. A motor home was luxury camping.

But he still wondered how he and Lisa would get along. They were superficially being nice to one another for the sake of Rose, but Sully knew that underneath their façade they were one word away from an argument.

But slowly Lisa was growing on him. He saw how sad she was over losing her sister. She'd sit on the garden bench and stare endlessly at the note from Carol and Rick, still not opening it.

Sometimes, he'd wanted to sit next to her and say a couple of comforting words, but then he decided that his sympathy wouldn't be welcome. Instead, he'd rope the statue, think and watch her out of the corner of his eye, pretending he didn't know she was crying.

He liked how she read books to Rose. She pointed to the pictures, asking her questions, and got her to make up her own stories.

He liked how she tried to cook, too. He saw the recipes she'd printed out from the Young Cooks website. Basic stuff. He supposed he ought to roll up his sleeves and do some cooking—he didn't mind at all—but he didn't want to seem like a know-it-all. She was doing fine.

Lisa climbed up the steps of the RV. "I think we're ready to go now. Oh-nine-thirty hours. Just as scheduled."

He didn't remember insisting on a time or a schedule.

"Then let's roll! Everyone buckle up." He pointed to the table with bench seats. "You can sit there, or someone can sit in the copilot's seat."

Lisa slid into the bench seat and Rose slid in opposite her. They both clicked on their seat belts.

He guessed that he'd be traveling without a copilot.

Nice and quiet. That was the way he liked it. Right?

This isn't a bad way to travel, Lisa thought as she tucked Rose into bed. She liked how the sides of the bed/kitchen table formed a barrier and secured Rose from rolling off. Traveling with a bathroom was another good perk.

But it still didn't beat flying.

Her cell phone rang, and she looked at the caller. It was her friend Luann at JFW Aviation. She was in charge of booking charters.

Her heart began to race and the blood started zinging through her veins at the thought of flying again. It had been too long.

"Hi, Luann! Got something for me?"

"Yeah, I do. I have a charter of high rollers going from Albany to Vegas. This would be perfect for you since you're somewhat near Albany already. It's just a quickie. You'll be back in three days."

"You want me to stay in Vegas?"

"Sure. It doesn't make sense for me to fly you back commercial and then send you back again the next day just so you can fly the charter back."

But she'd be gone for three days.

"When?" Lisa asked, pulling her appointment book and a pen from her purse. No electronics for her when it came to her appointments.

"Okay, got it." Lisa wrote down the information and blocked out the dates. "Should be no problem, but I'll let you know for sure. Thanks, Luann."

She was going to fly again! As she hurried toward the front of the RV to tell Sully, she felt like she was walking on sunshine.

Wait! A cloud blocked her sun when she remembered that the dates for the charter fell on a weekend. She'd told Sully that she'd fly during the week so he could ride on weekends. Now what? She didn't want to turn down her first charter, and it'd be round trip from Albany. Just what she'd wanted.

She had to discuss it with Sully.

Taking the passenger's seat, she turned toward him. "Where are we?"

"Pennsylvania. We're not as far as I thought. I forgot that Molly had to be walked, and I didn't know that Snowball would be barfing up hairballs."

"I'm the one cleaning up cat barf," she said. "Not you."

"And I'm the one walking around with plastic bags picking up dog poop."

Lisa chuckled. "I never thought I'd ever be doing this."

"Me, either." He picked up a bottle of water and took a big draw.

"Thank goodness we don't have to follow Rose around with a plastic bag," Lisa said.

Sully spewed his water all over the windshield and the front of his light blue shirt. His laughter bounced around the motor home. Lisa joined in.

When they both sobered up, they fell silent. Lisa watched the lines on the road flash by, and she was beginning to drift off to sleep. She yawned, then pinched her top lip to wake herself up.

"How about if I relieve you for a while?" she asked.

"You're too tired to drive."

"I guess I am. When can we quit?"

Sully pointed to the sign on the left that said "Sleepy Bear Campgrounds and RV Park."

"We can quit just as soon as I get a site and hook up the RV."

She yawned again. "Good."

He pulled the rig in front of the office, put the RV in Park and hurried down the steps behind Lisa's seat. "I'll be right back."

Lisa closed her tired eyes, thinking that she'd talk to Sully in the morning about the charter flight.

She must have dozed off because the next thing she heard was Sully talking on his cell.

"Of course I'll be there, Chet. Wouldn't miss it. Sure. I'll be glad to sign autographs at the Boot Yard. What's the date again? Got it. That's the Anaheim event? Two weeks from this weekend? Got it. No problem."

And she hadn't told Sully about it yet. Now he'd committed to an autograph signing.

Lisa sighed. If she remembered correctly what Sully had told her, the next event was the one event at which some cowboys would be dropped from the tour if they had low scores. Others would replace them. It was important for Sully to ride. He was high enough in the rankings to not worry about being dropped, but other riders were hot on his tail, trying to pass him in the standings. If a rider had a good day in the go-rounds, anything could happen.

She and Rose weren't going to follow Sully around like a couple of buckle bunnies. Rose needed stability, and that meant the big Victorian, not a home on wheels where she slept on the converted kitchen table for weeks at a time.

So far, Rose was having the time of her life. While Sully was driving, they'd played games, colored and put together puzzles on the table. She wanted Rose to have fun on this trip, to be a little girl without a care in the world, and so did Sully.

Now they were stopping at a park where there was an indoor pool, and Rose had put on her bathing suit fifty miles away in anticipation.

It was only seven-thirty at night, but all Lisa wanted to do was sleep. Yet it was time to be a mother and take Rose to the pool for a while.

She sure hoped that Sully brought his bathing suit, too.

Bonding. Wasn't that what she'd wanted on this trip?

They pulled into their campsite, and Sully hooked up whatever needed hooking up while she changed into a pair of shorts and a dark T-shirt to swim in. She didn't bring a bathing suit with her from Atlanta, never thinking that she'd need one, and didn't have time to go clothes shopping to any great extent.

Neither did Sully, although he found a pair of cutoffs. The three of them walked together to the indoor pool, hand-in-hand, with Rose between them. The stars were shining bright in the black sky and a full moon was smiling down on them.

Sully looked down at Rose, then at Lisa, and grinned. He winked. "What a beautiful night."

"Sure is."

"So we're going swimming, right, Rose?" Lisa asked.

"Yes! I want to swim!" She turned to Sully. "Will you go swimming with me, Uncle Sully?" Rose asked.

Why didn't Rose ask me to take her swimming?

"I sure will. All three of us are going swimming."

At least Sully included me.

"Yippee!" Rose yelled, suddenly jumping.

Sully and Lisa tightened their grip on her hand and caught her before she fell.

Just like real parents, Lisa thought.

A half hour later in the pool, Sully was supporting Rose as she splashed, making like she was swimming.

Sully turned to her, water dripping down his strong chest. His arms were thick with muscles, especially his riding arm. His disheveled hair glistened with beads of water, and she liked how he smiled. His whole face lit up.

She understood why the buckle bunnies found him sexy.

A sense of calm came over Lisa as she watched Sully play with their niece. He was good with Rose. Actually, he was like a kid himself.

She wondered how long it would take before he "forgot" his responsibilities and skipped out to party with his pals and a gaggle of groupies, like he was known to do.

Things were going great so far, but it was only day one.

Could Sully go the distance?

Could she?

Rose was safely tucked into the dinette bed. Molly the mutt was sleeping on the floor beside her, and Snowball was currently using the litter pan in the bathroom.

Rose had told them that she was going to say her night

prayers, and Sully silently gave Carol and Rick kudos for teaching her right.

"I want to pray for Mommy and Daddy in heaven. I hope they saw how good I was swimming. And I want to tell them that I'm going to Disney World."

Her prayers broke his heart, and he found himself at a loss for words. Rick would never see his little girl grow up. Would never see her graduate, get married or have children of her own.

It wasn't the first time he'd heard Lisa and Rose mention the theme park. He'd better take her, or he'd never forgive himself.

As Rose drifted off to sleep, he and Lisa sat on the seats in the front of the RV. He popped the top of a beer as Lisa drank a diet cola.

He took a long draw of his beer. Delicious. "You know, Lisa, you could have told me about your plans."

"I didn't have a chance. I just mentioned that we were going to Florida and would be near the park, and Rose took it from there. I'll have to be more careful about what I say."

"I'm not mad. I just feel bad that I didn't think of it myself. I'll work it in, even if I have to drive all night coming back home. It'll be worth it."

"That's really nice of you, Sully."

Her emerald eyes met his, and for a brief moment Sully thought that she actually liked him.

Nah!

He noticed Lisa unsuccessfully trying to stifle a yawn.

"You take the bed in back," he said. "I'll sleep on the floor."

"I couldn't take your bed, could I?"

Lisa tilted her head, almost flirtylike. He must be mistaken. Lisa was not the flirting type. She was too serious, too straight-laced. As a matter of fact, he thought she was a bit of a snob.

Obviously, she wanted the bed.

"I can handle the floor. I spent many days sleeping under the stars in Montana mostly during round-up. At least there's a carpet here."

Lisa seemed surprised by what he'd said. "I knew you were from Montana, but I didn't know you did real cowboy stuff."

"Bull riding isn't real cowboy stuff?"

"I think of it more like a sport," she said.

He shrugged. "You're right. Bull riding isn't something that occurs on a typical day on the ranch. I only got on bulls at the ranch to practice. Now I practice at my buddies' ranches. Someone always has a spread near the events."

Suddenly her eyes grew wide. "Wait a minute. You had a ranch?"

"Sure did. The Mountain View Ranch in Elsie, Montana. The best place in the world." He'd loved the place while he had it. "But I sold it to a buddy. Riding the PBR circuit, I was never there."

He and Sid Peterson had a handshake agreement. If Sid ever wanted to sell, Sully had first dibs on it, but that would never happen. Not now. Not when he had Rick's daughter to raise back at the big old Victorian in Salmon Falls, New York.

He sighed. If he ever went back to Montana now, it'd only be to visit.

"Funny, I never pictured you as the ranching type," Lisa said.

"Which means?" He raised an eyebrow.

"I guess I always had you pictured as tumbling tumbleweed."

"Just drifting along, huh? Just like you? Isn't that what our respective parents pointed out?" he asked.

She rolled her eyes. "I so want to prove to them that we can be good guardians to Rose."

"I know." But proving to his parents that he could do anything major like raising Rose seemed too much of a long shot. However, his brother Rick had been Gordon and Betsy Sullivan's pride and joy. A Wall Street millionaire, who didn't even have to work on Wall Street, he had been a total success. He'd even married the perfect woman. They'd adored Carol, and when Rick had put their first grandchild into their arms, he'd become even more perfect, if that was possible.

Sully could never be jealous of Rick. Rick was a great guy, a stand-up guy, a good-natured guy and a terrific big brother. Rick would have gone to the wall for him, and Sully would have returned the favor.

However, Brett Sullivan, second son, was a big disappointment to the Colonel and Mrs. Sullivan. He chose the cowboy lifestyle instead of a civil service job or the army. He did go to West Point briefly after high school, which got their hopes up, but he wasn't there long enough to unpack before he hitchhiked to the first PBR event.

He'd be considered by many to be a nomad, a rolling stone, a carefree cowboy who was doing what he wanted and living from go-round to go-round. His relationships with the opposite sex were mutually satisfying and perfectly shallow. That's the way he wanted it. Then he moved on.

How did that old country song go? Something about never loving a woman enough to stay—instead a cowboy saddles up and rides away.

"Sully?" Lisa said. "A penny for your thoughts?"

"They aren't worth that much."

"The day went well. Don't you think?" Lisa asked.

He knew that she wanted him to say yes.

"Sure. It was a great day. We didn't fight. Rose laughed a lot and enjoyed the long ride, mostly because you played with her. She loved splashing in the pool. And now she's sleeping like a three-year-old should."

"You were the one who made her laugh. I was the one who was making sure she didn't drown." Lisa yawned, then stood. "I'm still nervous about us raising her."

"You have to relax, Lisa. You hover over her too much."

"And you need to hover more!"

"Look, Lisa, anyone in their right mind would be nervous about raising children. We both love her, so it'll be easy. I think that confidence will come in time. If not confidence, then at least competence."

Her eyes grew large with surprise. "You are absolutely right about that!"

Her reaction made something in him wake up after a long sleep. Maybe he was lacking confidence and competence in his personal life. In his bull riding career, he'd always had plenty of both.

However, according to his parents, he had no track record of doing anything right.

So what made him think he could do right by Rose?

Chapter Four

Lisa never imagined that her life would consist of trips to the bathroom to assist her niece, playing dollies, feeding animals, picking up dog poop, cleaning a litter box and doing laundry. She looked forward to Rose's afternoon nap when there was a bit of time to just sit and read. Thank goodness for microwave meals. They were a blessing to the unskilled cook.

However, microwave meals weren't nutritious enough, so Lisa always made a nice salad and had plenty of fruit available. She'd even grilled hot dogs and hamburgers in the oven of the RV. She was pretty proud of herself that they were edible.

She walked to the front of the RV and sat down in the passenger's seat. She was just about to ask Sully if he'd like hot dogs again for dinner, but he spoke first.

"Three days on the road is enough. I'm going to drive all night. We'll roll into the arena in Fort Lauderdale in the morning," Sully announced while checking his GPS. "Then we can park this rig at the arena for the next two days."

"Park it where?"

"At the far end of the arena. The other guys and some of their families will be there in their RVs."

Lisa had heard all about how the cowboys circled their wagons, so to speak, and partied day and night. She wanted no part of that, and it wasn't appropriate for Rose.

"Have you lost your mind? Rose and I are not living on a parking lot." She kept her voice as low as she could so she didn't wake the little girl.

"But there will be children for Rose to play with and—"

"You never said anything about a parking lot. I thought we'd be camping at a campground like we've been doing," she whispered, but it was a loud whisper.

"I didn't think that it'd be—"

"That's right. You didn't think."

Sully kept on driving, but Lisa could see his white-knuckled grip on the wheel. She didn't care how mad he was.

Sully let out a loud breath. "I'm trying to tell you that the riders bring their families and there are children that Rose can play—"

"And there will be drinking and the buckle bunnies will be trolling, and…and…I don't want Rose subjected to all that. Nor do I want to be subjected to it!"

"You have it all wrong, Lisa. It's not like that. I—"

"This discussion is over."

"But we haven't discussed anything. You won't even let me talk."

"There's nothing more to say." Lisa shot the words at him like darts.

"Fine!" He said the word through gritted teeth. "I'll rent a car."

"Rent a car? Why?"

"So that I can get back and forth from the campground to the arena. You might want to rent a car, too. I'm sure that you don't want to go as early as I have to be there. Or you could drive this thing, but you'll have to unhook it from the utilities."

"Oh." She never thought of that. It was a possibility, but he'd have to show her how it was done. How hard could it be compared to a jet? Not that she ever had to do that kind of thing; that's what ground crews were for. "Where's the closest campground?"

He leaned over and pushed some buttons on his GPS. "It looks like the closest one is almost an hour away. I don't know if it has a pool for Rose and all the amenities that you require. I'll have to research them later. I'm a little busy driving."

She could detect the ragged edge of sarcasm in his voice. She didn't particularly want to drive in an unfamiliar city with Rose to find the darn arena from the campground.

"Maybe we could skip watching the bull riding," she suggested, even though she was dying to see the event in person. And Rose would probably never forgive her. All she talked about was "the big, mean bulls" that her uncle Sully rode and how she wanted to cheer for him.

He shrugged. "You could."

"But what would I tell Rose?"

"Tell her the truth. Tell her that you're too uptight to meet new people, people that might not be pilots or flight attendants or air traffic controllers. Tell her that you can't have fun in a place that's a gathering of people who are hard-working, salt-of-the-earth types."

Lisa swallowed hard. There might be some truth in what he said, but it made her seem so…shallow, so snobbish. She wasn't really like that. Was she? She was just thinking of Rose.

"Maybe I did jump to conclusions," she decided. "I should have let you talk."

"Boy howdy. You think?"

"First, tell me why you think I'm such a snob."

"Remember when Carol and Rick got married? All of the ladies in the wedding party and a lot of Carol's friends went to a male strip club. You didn't go."

"That's right."

"You announced to everyone that it was crass. Yes, I believe that was the word you used," he said.

"I think you're probably right."

"You threw a wet blanket on their fun. Carol and the rest of the ladies blew it off, but I could tell that Carol was very disappointed, sad even, that you wouldn't participate in her party."

Carol was disappointed? Sad? Was he right about that? She would have hated for Carol to feel that way.

"What should I have done? Gone with them even though I knew I'd have an awful time?"

"My point is that you assumed you'd have an awful time. Maybe you would have laughed and had the time of your life. Maybe you would have put the first dollar in the dancer's bikini briefs."

She grunted. "I doubt that."

"Well, you'll never know, will you?"

She remained silent, although she was ready to blast him. Where did the cowboy get the nerve to criticize her? Just because he was a party reptile and she wasn't didn't mean that she was a failure.

Just another example of how they are so different.

"Remember Rose's christening?" he asked.

"How could I forget? You hauled in a keg of beer and a box of cigars. All the men sat around drinking and smoking those smelly things and watching football."

"We smoked outside, so we didn't bother anyone."

"And you all were drinking like the world was ending," she said. "It was a christening party, for heaven's sake! Carol had planned a nice gathering *inside* the house."

"It was a nice gathering, and we did come inside."

"At halftime," she reminded him. "To eat. That's all. It would have been nice if we all could have sat and—"

"Talked each other to death?"

"Yes. I mean...no. All the guests could have had a nice conversation—together. Instead, it was like two separate parties—the women in the living room and the men on the patio."

"And you think that was my fault?"

"Absolutely."

"Because I brought the keg and the cigars."

"Correct." Now he was understanding her.

"But the Steelers were playing the Ravens that day," he said.

She let out an unladylike grunt. Sully was just trying to get her riled even more, and she walked right into it.

"You know, you could have passed up that wine in a box and joined us in a brew. Some of the women snuck out, including Carol, and pumped herself a beer. She even took a puff on Rick's cigar." He chuckled. "Now that's a real woman!" He glanced at her, then quickly turned back to look at the road. "But you never came out to the patio."

She turned to him, feeling like she had to stick up for herself. "It was Latour!" She was so frustrated that was all she could think of to say.

"Huh?"

"The wine. I brought Latour. And it wasn't in a box."

"Oh, fancy stuff."

"Forget it, Sully. Just forget it!" She was just about to head for bed when she turned back. "You know, we have

nothing in common except Rose. We're as different as…
Let me put this in terms you might understand…as different as a bull and a chicken. Carol and Rick were wrong in
picking the two of us."

"They were wrong in dying," he muttered.

"Drive to the parking lot of the Fort Lauderdale arena,"
she said slowly. "We'll stay there. However, as soon as I feel
that things are getting out of hand for Rose—and for myself—we are out of there."

"Yes, Colonel." He saluted. "Oh, sorry, Lisa. I thought I
was talking to my father for a moment."

Her mouth went dry. Was she really that bossy?

She was just about to call him something unflattering
but decided against sinking to his level.

She took a deep breath and tried to explain how she felt.
"I have a very serious job, Sully. I am responsible for the
lives of hundreds of people every time I fly. They have families and loved ones, and I don't want to make a mistake. I
don't have time for what you think is fun."

"Then what would you do for fun?" he asked.

Good question. She hadn't thought about that recently,
but she'd had an old dream from before she got her pilot's
license. "Ballroom dancing lessons."

She prepared herself for a big laugh from him.

"Ballroom dancing, huh?" he asked but didn't laugh. "So
what's stopping you?"

Someone to dance with, she thought. She had never had
the time to date. All she did was study. In high school, in
college and in flight school she drove herself to be the smartest, the best, the brightest. She wouldn't settle for anything
less. On the rare occasion when someone had dared to ask
her out, they never asked her again. Either her studiousness
or her seriousness drove them away.

In flight school, she was given several nicknames: Ice

Princess, Ice Pilot and Frigid Phillips—her personal favorite.

"Lisa?"

"What?"

"Did we just have a fight?"

"It sure seemed like a fight."

"From now on, could you just let me finish a sentence?" he asked gently. "We could have avoided all of this."

She took a deep breath. "I think we got some things off our chest—things that needed to be said."

"Maybe."

"It just shows how different we are," Lisa pointed out.

"Yeah."

"But I promise to let you finish a sentence." She laughed.

Sully snapped his fingers. "One more thing."

"Go ahead."

"Did you ever realize how much you are like my parents? Kind of rigid, inflexible, aloof—"

"How about stopping there?" she asked.

"Hey, you didn't let me finish my sentence!" He laughed. "You promised."

"Sully, since you started this topic of conversation, did you ever realize how much you are like my parents? Kind of unconventional, a maverick, a free spirit with no roots, a—" She stopped to take a breath. "Aren't you going to stop me?"

"Hell, no. I like what you said about me. Thanks for the compliments."

"You're just…impossible!"

"Thanks again!"

She smiled. She couldn't help herself; when Sully wasn't drinking, womanizing or otherwise being a jerk, he could be fun.

He was also insightful. She'd never realized that they

were like each other's parents until he'd pointed it out. They were rebels in their own different ways.

From what she knew about the Sullivans from Carol and by her own observations, she had to admit that he was probably right. She hated to admit it, but she was kind of similar to them.

Merciful heavens!

Maybe she did need some fun in her life. All she did was fly and sleep, preferably not at the same time.

Ha! She'd made a joke.

Maybe…just maybe…Sully was waking up a part of her that had been buried too long: her sense of humor.

"Sweet dreams," Sully said.

"If you'd let me drive this thing, I could take a turn."

"You stick to planes. I'll drive my rig."

"Good night, then."

She walked the six steps to check on Rose. She was still sleeping, as peaceful and as beautiful as an angel.

"I don't know how this is going to work, Rose, but it has to. We have to get along, your uncle Sully and me." She brushed a curl of soft brown hair from her niece's forehead. "For you, sweet girl. For you."

Sully was grateful for the silence. He had a lot on his mind: how to raise Rose, how to get along with Lisa, the current bull riding in Fort Lauderdale, how he could work the rest of the circuit, the Finals in Vegas and a partridge in a pear tree.

He hoped that there wouldn't be anything in the arena camping area that would cause Lisa to climb back onto her high horse.

Once in a while, he wished she'd let her hair down.

They hadn't been in each other's company very much—only when Rick and Carol had a major event. Like Rick's bachelor's party that he'd arranged. Everyone was still talk-ing about that wild bash. He'd rented a suite at a large hotel in Albany, and they'd partied all night long.

He remembered Lisa tearing him apart the next morning. He'd had a doozy of a hangover, and he'd made the mistake of opening the door of the suite.

He'd had to walk over Rick and several more snoring bodies to get to the door.

He'd looked through the peephole. Lisa.

What a mistake it had been to open the door for her.

She wouldn't stop yelling at him. Through the boozy haze of his brain, he gathered that he and Rick had overslept and were supposed to be at some kind of Jack and Jill shower that Lisa had arranged at the same hotel's outdoor patio.

"Rick was supposed to be there at eleven-hundred hours," she yelled, pointing to her watch.

She always yelled and pointed to her watch.

"Quiet, please," he remembered saying to Lisa. "I'll get Rick there. Just stop talking."

Lisa finally left, and he got Rick on his feet, walked him into the shower, clothes and all, and turned the cold water on. Then Sully made coffee, wrapped Rick's hand around the cup and made him take a drink.

"I want to die," Rick said, slumped against a shower wall. "Just let me die."

"No can do, bro. You have a shower—the gift kind of shower—to attend with your beloved fiancée downstairs. If I don't get you to it, I'll be the one who's dead."

Sully had finally delivered Rick to the patio, looking presentable and almost lifelike. Carol had smiled and took Rick's hand, and they disappeared into the crowd.

Unfortunately, Lisa then appeared. She'd looked him over, from his scuffed boots to his dusty black cowboy hat. In between, he wore beat-up, but clean, jeans and a new long-sleeved chambray shirt with the PBR logo. He'd just slipped it out of the plastic wrap.

He had glanced at the crowd. Even their yuppie garden-party attire couldn't have embarrassed him enough to put on a golf shirt and a pair of khaki pants, even if he owned them.

Besides, Brett Sullivan didn't get embarrassed.

He'd supposed that Lisa Phillips looked nice enough with a white dress with colorful flowers all over it. It was cinched at the waist with a gold belt and then flared out, making her legs look…well, really good. Her hair was twisted up, but wispy curls of blond hair had escaped and framed her face in gold. Whenever they'd met before, he'd noticed that she wasn't bad-looking but, man, she was the ultimate snob.

How could Carol and Lisa be sisters when Carol was so laid-back, sweet and normal?

Lisa had stared a hole through him with her dark green eyes. "I suppose I should thank you for getting Rick here, but if you men could tell time, I wouldn't have had to go to your hotel room."

Just what he'd needed—a lecture from Miss Perfect. Her words had been loud and noisy and shot right to his throbbing head.

"Shh," he said with his index finger over his mouth. "Why are you shouting?"

"I'm not shouting," she had said, then added under her breath, "I haven't met a man yet who could hold his liquor."

With a toss of her head, she'd turned and headed for his mother. He'd watched as she walked away from him, her white high heels making a clacking sound on the cement.

"Hmm…nice legs," he'd mumbled, looking around for coffee.

That was then. Now he was with Miss Perfect in a motor home headed for bull riding in Fort Lauderdale. With them was Rick and Carol's three-year-old daughter. He couldn't even think ahead to what was in store for him or them.

Damn! He wondered if they should have told the lawyer that they were traveling. Mr. Randolph had said he would make some unannounced visits. It might look to him like they'd all just picked up and left.

"Sully?"

He jumped, jarred out of his thoughts, as Lisa approached the front seat.

"I thought you were sleeping."

"I tried, but I didn't want to leave you alone here. You have to be tired, too. You've been driving since we left Sleepy Sheep Campground."

"Riding on the PBR circuit, I'm used to driving around the clock. Sometimes I drive across country alone, but sometimes I pick up some other riders along the way, and we take turns driving."

She wore black stretchy pants and a red tank top. Her feet were bare, but he noticed that her toenail color matched her tank top. She looked as cute as a newborn calf, although if he said that out loud, she'd have a fit.

She slipped into the passenger's seat and crossed her legs. He'd just been thinking of those legs, and wished he could see more of them.

"I told you several times that I'd drive. Why won't you let me?"

He shrugged. "I'd rather you take care of Rose."

"You need to take care of Rose, too."

"I do. Don't I take her on my walk arounds?"

"Yes. You do. But what about the daily stuff? You should be getting her washed and dressed, making sure she brushes her teeth and then doing it all in reverse at night. In between, there's keeping her busy and out of trouble and harm's way. And you always have to teach her—academics, rules for proper living, how to get along in society, societal norms, all kinds of things."

Rules? Society? Norms? For heaven's sake, it sounded like prison.

"I want Rose to have an easy, laid-back life. No pressure. Relaxed. Childhood should be fun."

Lisa took a deep breath. "Kids need discipline, responsibility, rules and stability."

"Kids need two things—fun and love."

"That's part of it, but they need so much more."

"And they need education so they can learn and find friends. But I still consider that love and fun," he conceded.

"But there's discipline in school, and rules and stability," Lisa insisted.

"Or Rose can be homeschooled. We can do that. We can take her on trips in the RV. She can learn so much by visiting places and talking to people," he said.

"Talking to strangers?" she asked, the shock evident in her voice.

"They wouldn't be strangers for long. Besides, we'll be with her."

"You sound like my parents, Sully." She crossed her arms, and he heard her breathing heavily. It almost sounded like she was trying not to cry. "We have to talk more about this. I didn't expect that we'd be this far apart on how to raise Rose."

He did. He'd known it since Rick and Carol had asked them both to be guardians. Of course, he'd never thought it'd happen in a million years.

Damn that slick road, that car they drove, the weather, the bridge and whatever the hell else he could throw in.

"Do you think that we can come to an agreement?" she asked.

"It might take a team of lawyers or maybe even the Supreme Court to make us agree, and even then we'd probably choose to go to prison rather than give in." He chuckled.

"But I thought we agreed to try because we love Rose."

"Yes, we love Rose."

"See? We have a good start!"

Maybe he was tired, after all, or maybe it was because Lisa thought about him enough to skip sleep and talk to him as he drove, but he had to agree.

"I'm going to promise to do my best to compromise with you, Lisa."

"I'll let you finish your sentences." She chuckled. "And let's try not to fight in the process."

Sully thought of their earlier fight, if you'd call it that. He'd call it verbal sparring. Neither of them got ugly, but they got plenty of things on the table in record time. He was a meat-and-potatoes kind of guy. He didn't like tiptoeing around important matters.

Lisa was pushy and overbearing and always wanted her own way, and...oh hell, she had great legs.

"Not fight? That I can't promise."

Chapter Five

"Lisa?"

She heard her name being called. The voice sounded vaguely familiar and very distant.

"Hey, Lisa! Wake up. We're in Fort Lauderdale, and we're pulling into the parking lot. You might want to disappear into the back and put some clothes on."

The sun was peeking under her eyelids, and she didn't want to open them.

"Hmm?"

"At least straighten up a bit," Sully said, and she could hear the teasing in his low, sexy voice. "I mean, I like the eye candy, but this is one big window and there are a lot of people around already. It looks like we're just in time for breakfast."

She opened her eyes a bit and looked down. She was slumped in the seat, and her tank top was—oh, dear—off center and her left breast was one centimeter shy of being completely exposed.

When she looked out, she saw dozens of people sitting at picnic tables and lined up at a buffet.

Quickly she fixed her top, grateful that Sully had slowed down. As fast as her numb legs would carry her, she twisted out of the seat and headed for the back.

Rose was just awakening from her sleep and she began to whimper.

"Mommy?"

Rose sat up in bed, thumb in her mouth. Tears ran down her face.

"It's Aunt Lisa, sweetie." She reached for a roll of paper towels behind her. Pulling off one, she dabbed at Lisa's cheeks. "Shh…you're okay."

"Uncle Sully?"

Lisa pointed. "He's right up there parking the motor home." Lisa made a face and put her finger over her lips. "Oops…I goofed. Uncle Sully calls this big thing his 'rig.' Uncle Sully is parking his rig."

Rose giggled, and that was just the reaction Lisa was hoping for.

"How about if you go to the bathroom, and we'll get dressed and meet all of Uncle Sully's friends?"

"The bull riders? Like Uncle Sully?"

"That's right, Rose," Sully said from up front. "You know some bull riders, don't you? Your mom and dad told me that you watch me on TV. You'll meet the other bull riders now, and some of them have little girls your age that you can play with. Is that cool?"

"Cool," Rose said, swiping her face with the sleeve of her flowery nightgown. "I have to go to the bathroom now. And I want my big girl panties."

The motor home came to a stop, and Lisa saw Sully waving out the large windshield.

"Sure," Lisa said, helping her get up from her bed. "Let's get ready."

"I'll be right back," Sully said, climbing out of the driver's side door. "I'll find coffee and bring you back a cup."

"I'd be eternally grateful."

Lisa got Rose ready for the day, changed her bed back into the dinette and popped a cartoon into the DVD for her to watch while she ate her cereal.

Lisa left the door of the bedroom open a crack while she dressed so she could keep an eye on Rose.

Sully arrived several minutes later with two white foam cups.

Coffee. Finally.

He sat opposite Rose in the dinette. "There's a little girl named Lacy who wants to play with you, Rose. She has a Mary doll just like yours and she has a dollhouse."

Rose slid out of the dinette and stood. "Can I go now and play with her?"

"Whoa! Finish your breakfast first, honey. Lacy is eating breakfast right now, too. There's plenty of time for you two to play, and her momma said that she'd take you both to the playground."

Playground? What an excellent idea. At least the girls wouldn't be playing in a parking lot.

She was grateful to Sully for arranging a playmate for Rose. She needed to be around kids her own age, but, of course, he never thought of her safety, especially around cars.

Lisa finished applying her makeup, then looked over her shoulder to see her reflection in the mirror hanging on the door of the closet.

When she opened the bedroom door and walked out, Sully raised both eyebrows and grinned.

"What?" Lisa asked.

"You look like you're ready for a walk on the red carpet, not a rodeo," Sully said.

Rose bounced in her seat. "You look pretty, Aunt Lisa. Doesn't she look pretty, Uncle Sully?"

Lisa held her breath. She didn't want him to answer that question. She didn't care about his opinion of her looks. She just wanted him to think that she was a good caretaker of Rose. She was just about to change the subject when he said, "Yes. Yes, your aunt Lisa does look pretty." He boldly stared at her from the top of her hair, which she'd tamed into submission with mousse, to the tip of her designer sandals.

Her cheeks heated as she met Sully's gaze. She couldn't remember the last time she'd blushed at a compliment, but her face was currently on fire. Sully thought she was pretty and for some reason she felt like she was in free fall.

"Don't you have jeans and a T-shirt, though?" he asked. "I think you'd be more comfortable."

The rosy-pink glow faded. Lisa pulled the cord on her parachute and landed squarely on solid ground.

"I'm comfortable." She took a deep breath. "Besides, I don't have jeans and my other shoes are heels. I haven't exactly had time to go shopping, you know! This is a DKNY blouse and the slacks are from the new collection of a designer that I met in New York City, C. Z. Bofino."

"I'm sure all those initials mean something important, but here, at the bull riding, all you need is a pair of Wranglers and a T-shirt." He handed her one of the foam cups. "I'll be right back. I know where the merchandise is. I'll shop for you."

"You'll what?" Lisa stood in the middle of the motor home, not believing her ears.

"Turn around," he said twirling his finger in a circle.

"I will not."

He walked around her with his hand on his chin. "Okay. I think I know your jean size. What size shoe do you wear?"

Lisa rolled her eyes. "You are not buying me clothes!"

"What's your shoe size?" he asked again.

"Eight."

"Trust me," he said, leaving by the side door.

Lisa sat in the spot that he'd just vacated. "Your uncle Sully is too much," she mumbled more to herself than Rose.

Rose was too busy watching cartoons and eating her cereal to pay her much attention, so Lisa looked out the window at the riders and their families milling around the RVs.

Without exception, they all wore jeans.

It was then that Lisa realized that Sully wasn't concerned about her being comfortable. He was concerned about his friends being comfortable around *her*.

Obviously, stepping out of his RV dressed like she was ready for a cocktail party wasn't going to cut it with this crowd.

It wasn't that she was putting on airs or being intentionally insensitive. She truly didn't bring a lot of clothes with her.

She had jeans, but they were all back at her apartment in Atlanta. And she only wore a T-shirt when she jogged.

She couldn't imagine wearing a shirt with an illustration of a rearing bull on her chest all day long.

Did that make her a snob?

Sully walked back into the RV with his arms full of bags and boxes.

He walked into the bedroom and put everything on the bed. "Try this stuff on."

Walking into the bedroom as he walked out, she shut the door behind him. Picking up the folded denim, she shook them out. There was that Wrangler patch. This was like high school, and she was trying to fit in.

She slipped her slacks off and stepped into the heavy denim. Zipping up the zipper and snapping the snap, she stood and looked in the mirror. Not bad!

Off went the designer blouse as she picked up a T-shirt. Shoot! A screaming yellow shirt. Just what she'd wanted! She put it on and tucked it in. Next came a black belt with shiny silver conchos and turquoise. She liked that a lot.

The next box contained a pair of leather boots with a green saguaro cactus on both sides. At the base was a howling wolf. In the background was a full moon.

She slipped them on. She would never have picked them out herself, but for some reason, she liked them. And they fit!

Sully was incredible. Had he been around that many women that he knew women's sizes?

Opening the bedroom door, she walked out. She was greeted with a long, low wolf whistle from Sully.

"Looking good, Lisa."

"You are pretty, Aunt Lisa."

Lisa bent over to give Rose a kiss on the forehead. "Thanks, sweetie."

"Let's go meet everyone and grab some breakfast," Sully said with his hand on the door.

"Should I bring something?" Lisa asked, mentally taking inventory as to what she had to contribute.

"Not this time. And don't worry about lunch. I'll make a big pot of chili."

He took Rose's hand and helped her down the stairs. Then he raised his hand to assist Lisa.

"I'm okay," she said, listening to her new boots clunking down the stairs.

They were greeted with smiles, hugs and high fives. Lisa

noticed immediately that Sully was well-liked and that any friend of Sully's was a friend of theirs.

Rose got a lot of hugs, and the little girl grinned. Then her playmate Lacy arrived with a princess doll in one hand and a pink tote shaped like a castle in the other.

The two girls, instant friends, went off to play on a picnic table. Lisa and Sully followed, taking seats near the girls.

"Help yourself to the buffet," Lacy's mother, Darlene, said. "I'll watch the girls."

"Thank you," Lisa said, glancing at Sully.

"Don't worry," Sully whispered. "Darlene will take good care of Rose. And we're only going over there." He pointed to the buffet tables about ten yards away. "We have to stop hovering. We're going to give her a complex."

"We're not hovering—we're watching her. She's only three, Sully."

"You know what I mean," he said.

It took a half hour to reach the buffet. Everyone wanted to talk to Sully. He shook hands with their kids and signed autographs. He ruffled the hair of boys, tipped his hat to the girls and tickled the feet of babies.

In spite of him not wanting to hover over Rose, she noticed that he was always glancing over at the little girl and seemed ready to sprint to her at a moment's notice.

Her heart warmed to him. They might have their differences, but so far he was a great caretaker for Rose, and he obviously enjoyed all kids.

They helped themselves to pancakes that Silvano Perez, a Brazilian rider, was cooking on a grill hooked up to a generator. There were muffins, bagels and a variety of fruit and cereal on the table.

As they were sitting at a table eating, a tall, thin cowboy approached with a brown gear bag over his shoulder and a toothpick hanging from his lips.

"Look what the wolves dragged in," he said to Sully, then slapped him on the back.

"Look what the wolves didn't want. Hi, Tate." Sully turned to her. "Lisa, this is Tate—"

"Porter. I know. I've seen him on TV." Lisa held out her hand. "Nice to meet you in person." He was more handsome in real life, she noticed.

"Tate, this is Lisa Phillips, my sister-in-law."

Tate tweaked the brim of his hat and shook her hand. "Woo-hee! Sully, where did you find this angel?"

She could listen to his Texas drawl all day.

"In Salmon Falls, New York," Sully answered.

"What were you doing in New York?" Tate asked, still holding Lisa's hand.

"Long story. I'll tell you over a case of Lone Star."

Tate laughed. "I'm looking forward to that." With an extra shake, he let go of her hand.

"Are you two traveling together?" the cowboy asked Lisa.

She nodded. "With our niece, Rose. She's playing with a little girl named Lacy." She pointed. "Over there at the picnic table."

Tate grinned. "My Lacy sure loves to play with her dolls."

"Lacy's your daughter?"

"One of them. I have five sweet girls: Sarah, Jennifer, Melissa, Julie and Lacy. Six sweet girls, if you count Darlene, and I do."

"He's been busy," Sully said. "And he just won't leave Darlene alone."

"I gotta get me at least one cowboy. So we keep trying." Tate laughed.

Just then four dark-haired girls came running to Tate, hugging his waist and legs, wherever they could reach according to their height. Laughing, he sat down, cross-legged, as the girls climbed all over him.

"Let's go get your mother and take a walk over to the playground. What do you say?" Tate asked.

A cheer went out from the girls, and they walked together toward Darlene.

"I'll get Rose," Lisa said to Sully, tossing her empty paper plate into a plastic garbage bin. "We can take Molly for a walk around the neighborhood."

"Let Rose come with us," Tate shouted over his shoulder. "We'll keep an eye on her. Why don't you two relax for a while? You just rolled in."

Darlene approached the group with Rose and Lacy. "What's up, Tate?"

"We're going to the playground!" the girls shouted.

More kids gathered and more parents around the group. Soon a huge group was going to the playground.

Sully knelt down to talk to Rose. "Do you want to go to the playground with Lacy and her mom and dad?"

Rose grinned. "Yes!"

"Sweetie, I thought I'd try and take a nap before the bull riding. I'm a little tired," Sully said.

Lisa had almost forgotten that Sully drove all night and hadn't slept. He certainly needed some rest. He had to be his best for the event tonight.

"I'll go with you, Darlene," Lisa said. "I can't leave you with all the kids, and—"

"Lisa, you look a little tired yourself. Go catch some rest," Darlene said. "Tate will help me."

Lisa looked at the RV. Sully had released the awning and there was a nice patch of shade. She'd love to stretch out on a lawn chair and close her eyes for a while.

"If you're sure you and Tate can handle the kids, I'd love to sit a while without moving," Lisa said.

Several women had overheard their conversation and stopped.

One of the women, wearing a T-shirt that said "Cowboys do it in eight seconds," smiled at her.

"Going to bull riding events with our guys is like being at one big block party without the booze," she said. "We keep an eye on each other's kids, and we're just one big happy family."

"Only we're not dysfunctional!" said a woman pushing a stroller.

"It's like a commune here!"

Lisa's stomach roiled.

"Yeah," Darlene agreed. "I never thought about it that way, but we travel together, eat together, watch everyone's kids and whatever. Hey, we're the cowboy commune."

Commune?

Over her dead body!

Lisa flashed back to a long dormitory with rows of bunk beds. She was always on the top bunk, and Carol always took the bottom. Lisa had lived in fear that she'd fall out of bed, so she'd spent most of the night listening to everyone snore and trying not to move on her thin mattress.

Every day had been the same as the other. School was optional, and playing was encouraged. White was the dress of the day, day after day, gauzy, billowy white.

She attended school faithfully. On many days, she was the only one there. But even school was different from what she longed for. She wanted orderly rows of desks; instead she learned her lessons while sitting on the grass or hiking in the woods. And she never had the same teacher two days in a row.

At the end of the school day, she couldn't wait to see her parents. Unfortunately, they were always busy—planting, harvesting, cooking, drumming, singing, dancing.

Lisa had longed for a schedule, a routine, some kind of order and organization. She even remembered making up her own schedule until one of the parents found it and tore it up, telling her that she should enjoy her childhood and that schedules were for those who were slaves to the clock.

One of the reasons Lisa enjoyed being a pilot was the fact that she lived by schedules and timetables.

Now a sense of déjà vu slammed into her, and her throat felt too dry to swallow. Lisa took Rose's hand. "We'll meet you all at the playground. I have to…um…go back to the RV."

Her voice sounded scratchy to her own ears, and she didn't miss the looks that were exchanged before she left.

I'm not a snob. Really, I'm not, she thought before she hurried back to the motor home. She helped Rose up the stairs, then walked in behind her.

Sully was shirtless and shoeless, wearing only a pair of cutoff jeans. She wondered if he usually slept in his underwear but put on the cutoffs as a concession to them.

And she knew he wore white briefs because she'd seen them in the laundry basket.

On any other date and time, she might better appreciate how buff he looked, but bitter memories of the Happy Life Commune were foremost in her mind.

She tried to remain calm, but she wanted to jump behind the wheel and drive away from the…uh…block party.

She didn't know why the woman's words had gotten to her, and she knew she was overreacting, but she couldn't stop herself.

"Sully, I can't do this. Please take us to a campground. I can't live in a cowboy commune."

Chapter Six

"I gotta go potty."

"Go ahead, Rose. Yell if you need help," Lisa said.

Sully waited until his niece closed the door to the bathroom. "Sit down, Lisa, and tell me what's got you upset," Sully said.

"I just want to go to a campground."

"C'mon, Lisa, talk to me. What's this about a cowboy commune?"

She sat on the dinette bench. "Sully, you know my background. My parents are hippies left over from the sixties. I grew up in communes, and I hated that kind of life. Carol embraced it, but I didn't."

He sat down opposite her. "Carol must have known that about you."

"Of course she did," Lisa said softly. "And I'll never understand why she trusted me to be Rose's guardian."

"Trusted *us,*" Sully said. "Do you think that Rick and

Carol might have answered that question in the letter the lawyer gave us?"

Lisa lowered her eyes. "I'm not ready to open it yet, Sully. I'll know when." She looked at him, and handed him the envelope. "It's addressed to you, too. If you want to read the letter, go ahead."

He looked at the envelope, but didn't make a move to take it.

"When you think that the time is right, we'll open it together," he finally said.

She seemed relieved. "Thank you. That's really nice of you."

He winked. "I have my moments."

Lisa smiled. "I guess you do."

Suddenly completely exhausted, he rubbed his hands over his face to wake himself up. It was getting harder and harder to keep his eyes open.

"I'm going to help Rose take a bath," Lisa said.

He nodded. "Be careful of using too much water. We're pretty low."

"Okay."

He slid between the sheets of his bed. He could smell Lisa's flowery scent clinging to the linens.

He closed his eyes, needing to drift off into sweet sleep, when the door swung back open and Lisa stuck her head in.

"I have to get some clothes for Rose," she whispered. "For some reason, she suddenly decided she didn't want to go to the playground now, she wanted to take a shower." She shrugged.

He propped himself up on his forearms to watch her. "Go ahead. Get what you need."

He liked watching Lisa. There was scarcely a wasted movement when she was doing something, but right now she was double-tracking, dropping things, getting flustered.

"Can I help you find something?" he asked.

"If I knew that we were going to share the bed, I would have changed the sheets," she said. "I mean, we're not sharing the bed, not in the literal sense, but we are sharing the bed, somewhat…sharing…the…bed. We are separately sharing the bed. I guess that's what I'm trying to say."

Sully had never seen her so flustered, and he noticed that she avoided looking directly at him. But she was staring at his chest.

"I was going to sleep on the floor or fix up the dinette, but I didn't think you'd mind if I just used the bed for now," he explained.

"Um…I—I don't." Now her eyes were fixated on the ceiling. "I'll be out of here in a second." Her cheeks looked a little flushed. "I just can't find Rose's panties."

Well, she wouldn't find them on the ceiling.

He pointed. "What are those pink things in your hand?"

"Oh. Oh, yes. There they…are. Here they are."

Sully rubbed a hand over his chest, just scratching an itch. He thought he heard Lisa's breath catch, but he must have imagined it because her attention was now focused on the carpet.

"Well, I'd better see to Rose's shower." She bumped into the door and dropped some of the clothes that were in her hands. "Oh!"

He flipped off the sheet, jumped up and bent down to pick them up for her.

"I got it!" she said. "Stay in bed."

But he was already standing toe-to-toe with her in the small quarters. He was wearing his cutoff jeans and dammit if they weren't getting snug. Lisa was fully dressed, clutching Rose's pink underwear to her breast.

He handed her the rest of the clothes.

"Good night again…uh, Sully."

"G'night."

He opened the door for her, and as she backed through it, she finally met his eyes.

He closed the door behind her and practically dove into bed. Man, he was tired.

He stretched out, thinking of Lisa. What the hell was wrong with her? She wasn't acting like the efficient, confident, task-oriented pilot that she usually was.

She'd been a frazzled mess.

But then what accounted for Lisa's strange behavior?

He put his hands under his head, thinking.

He'd been around enough to tell when a lady was interested in him, and he'd bet his lucky bull rope that Lisa was interested.

Sully drifted off to sleep thinking of ways to test his hypothesis.

Lisa didn't mind the spray from the shower as she washed the soapy bubbles down the drain. She should turn up the cold water; it might cool off her cheeks.

Why was she acting like a schoolgirl?

In approximately the eighth grade, she'd had a crush on the big basketball star of the commune's half-hearted attempt at an organized sports team. His name was Kip Mc-Cleary, and he hadn't yet grown into his feet. The first to have a bountiful case of acne, poor Kip was forced to brandish a homemade cream that his mother and some of the other women had made. Kip's face had a purple hue.

But whenever there was a basketball game and half of the boys had to take off their shirts, she'd always hope that Kip would be on the shirtless team. There was always something so exciting and forbidden about seeing a man shirtless, especially at the commune, where gauzy white was the uniform for everyone.

Kip McCleary was a mere shadow when compared to Brett Sullivan. Brett had a body that made her gasp.

There wasn't an ounce of fat on his frame. His arms were thick with muscle and sinew, especially his riding arm. He had a smattering of dark hair that disappeared into the waist-band of his low-riding cutoffs.

Lisa splashed some water on her face. She had to get back to reality, and reality was the fact that the two of them were worlds apart as to how to raise Rose.

Oh, sure, Sully had a great body, he exuded masculine energy and he was starting to grow on her. Like a barnacle, she scoffed.

Shutting off the water, she wrapped a fluffy pink towel around Rose. The little girl kept singing away, a mishmash of cartoon theme songs.

Rose wrapped her arms around Lisa's neck, and Lisa could smell the scent of soap, shampoo and little girl. Lisa vowed to remember this moment, a moment when a bath, complete with bubbles, made a little girl happy.

"Thanks for the hug, sweetie."

"Can I play with Lacy now?"

"Sure. We'll go to the playground, but let's get you dressed first."

"Okay."

She helped Rose get dressed, and Rose sat down at the dinette as the DVD of a purple dragon caught her eye. Lisa went back to straighten out the bathroom.

She noticed by the overflowing laundry bag hanging on the back of the doorknob that she needed to do a wash. There must be a Laundromat somewhere around here.

It was Sully's turn to do laundry, but he needed to sleep. Then he had to get to the arena and ride. A large autograph session for the fans was scheduled after the event, so he wouldn't get back to the RV until very late.

Oh, she'd just do the darn laundry. He could do it the next time.

There was a knock on the door, and Lisa hurried to answer it. She wasn't ready for company. Her hair was wet and so was the front of her shirt. She needed to refresh her makeup, too.

Nevertheless, she swung the door open and found five giggling women. They were dressed in tight jeans, shirts with plunging necklines, boots and cowboy hats. They sported rhinestones, feathers, silver conch belts and big hair.

In Florida?

"Yes?" Lisa asked.

"Um…uh…we're here to see Sully. Is he here?" said a tall, tanned blonde. Whenever she moved her eyes, her bangs moved with them.

"Yeah, Sully," said another girl. She blew a bubble with her gum. "He's hot."

"Who are you?" said a third.

"I'm Lisa Phillips. I'm a friend of his. He's busy right now and can't come to the door. I'm afraid you'll have to wait and see him at the bull riding."

Rose peeked out under Lisa's arm. "Hi!"

"Who's that?" said a woman with glittery eyeliner. "There's nothing about kids in Sully's biography."

"I guess he needs an updated biography," Lisa said just to tweak the women. "Have a great day. Bye now." She had her hand on the outside door, ready to swing it shut.

"But—"

"Hey, wait a minute!"

"We want to see Sully."

Behind the buckle bunnies, Lisa noticed several fast-approaching security guards. "Ladies, I think you'd better boot scoot."

"Can't we see Sully? Just for a second," whined the blonde.

Lisa shook her head. "He'll be at the autographing after the event." She felt like Sully's agent.

Two security guards herded the women out of the area, while the other stayed and apologized to her. "Sorry, Mrs. Sullivan. It won't happen again."

It took her a while to find her voice. "Mrs.? Who? What?" She swallowed. "Oh, no. No! I'm not Mrs. Sullivan. Never. Never will I be Mrs. Sullivan."

The security guard shifted on his feet. "Sorry. Um…"

"Lisa Phillips."

"Sorry, Miz Phillips."

"Thanks for getting rid of the groupies," Lisa said, changing the subject.

He tipped his hat and hurried away. He probably thought she was a psycho after her overreaction to being called Mrs. Sullivan.

Poor man.

She closed the door and pondered why she reacted so strongly. She decided that Sully was driving her to the brink of insanity, and he didn't even know it. But it was all his fault.

"Can I go and play with Lacy now?" Rose asked.

Lisa would just like a moment to get herself together and fix her makeup, and maybe have another cup of coffee.

Instead, she wrote a note to Sully: "Going to the playground with Rose. Will you find out where there's a Laundromat? See you at the arena. Tickets? Good luck. Lisa."

Rose packed up her dolls, and they headed out of the RV. Rose handed the dolls to Lisa so she'd be free to skip.

Lisa noticed that the communal breakfast was over and lunch was not yet under way. She hoped that she wasn't the talk of the camping area due to her previous quick exit.

Rose spotted Lacy and was ready to scamper off to the little girl's trailer, but Lisa hurriedly grabbed her hand.

"Wait for me, Rose," Lisa called.

Lacy held up her doll. "My brother ran over Peggy with his skateboard, and her head fell off," Lacy said. "But my mommy put it back on."

Darlene, Lacy's mother, turned the corner. "I was just going to walk over to your RV. We're going back to the playground. How about if I take the girls now?"

"I was just going to ask you the same thing, only I was going to take the girls."

"I'd be glad to do it."

"Well, then that leaves laundry duty for me. Would you happen to know where I could do that?" Lisa asked.

"Right around the block." She pointed. "That way. It's an easy walk, even with a laundry basket. But take Lacy's wagon. It'll be easier for you."

"I'll take you up on that wagon. Thanks." Lisa didn't have many close friends due to her work schedule, but she felt that she could be friends with Darlene.

Unfortunately she'd only see Darlene during bull riding events.

Lisa sighed. She missed Carol so much. She would pick up the phone anytime day or night and talk to her sister. She still found herself reaching for the phone to tell Carol of something cute that Rose had done. Actually, she almost dialed Carol's phone number to tell her about Rose's singing in the shower.

As she walked back to Sully's RV pulling Lacy's red wagon, she waved to all those who made eye contact with her. Everyone was very friendly, and it made her feel less like a stranger.

They were friends who liked to share meals together, who liked to meet at bull riding events and catch up.

For some strange reason, she now wanted to belong.

Why? She was so unlike them. They were easygoing; she was uptight. They wore logo shirts and Western wear; she wore designer clothes. They had their boots planted firmly on the ground; she'd rather fly.

And they were just three reasons that she was so different from Sully.

She climbed up the metal stairs and unlocked the door. She could hear Sully's even snoring through the thin walls. Going into the bathroom, she got the laundry bag and a red plastic bottle of detergent.

Just as she was about to leave the bathroom, Sully blocked her way. His eyes were slitted, and he was rubbing the stubble on his chin.

"Lisa?"

She was staring at his washboard stomach, but she forced herself to meet his half-closed eyes.

"I'm going to do laundry. It's around the block. I have a red wagon to carry it all in." Why was she babbling about a wagon?

"A red wagon? That's nice," he mumbled.

"It's Lacy's wagon. She and Rose are at the playground. Darlene and Tate and the others are watching them, so I thought I'd do laundry."

"That's nice of you." He rubbed his eyes. "I'll cook up a pot of chili to bring to lunch. We can eat with the gang before I have to go to the arena. Is that all right with you?"

"Lunch with the gang?" she asked.

"Is that okay? I know you don't like to eat with everyone because it reminds you of the commune, but—"

"No. I'm fine."

He didn't say anything, but his deep-blue eyes opened a little wider.

"I'm fine, Sully. Really. It'll be fun."

"Okay. I'll start browning the beef," he said, "and then I'll jump in the shower."

The image of Sully shedding his cutoffs and letting the water sluice over his muscular body as he soaped up made Lisa's cheeks heat. When was she going to get over her girlish reaction to him?

Maybe it was because Sully was in such close proximity in the little RV. And she hadn't had sex in ages. First, she'd had a grueling flying schedule, and then, well, no one had interested her.

"I'll see if I can find a bakery in my travels," she said. "I'll get some nice bread to go with your chili."

"Sounds like a plan." He picked up the laundry bag and the soap, walked down the three metal steps in his bare feet and put it all in the wagon. Then he handed her a twenty.

"Thanks." She stuffed the bill into her pocket. "Well, I'd better get going and head to the Laundromat."

"Lisa?"

"Yes?"

"I want to thank you."

"For?"

"For doing such a good job with Rose and for the laundry and all."

"Thanks." His compliment made her feel all warm and fuzzy inside. Merciful heavens, she hadn't felt all warm and fuzzy in ages. "But I notice that you didn't mention my cooking."

"Your microwaving is top-notch." He made a goofy face and the "good" sign with his thumb and index finger, then he got serious. "We're doing fine. We'll get through this."

"Until Rose turns eighteen?"

"And beyond," he said.

Rose was three years old, so she figured that meant that she had fifteen years with Brett Sullivan.

Fifteen years. Somehow that didn't seem as bad as it had before.

Could there be hope for them yet?

Chapter Seven

Sully opened all the windows in the RV, set the air conditioner several degrees lower, took out his biggest frying pan and began cooking several pounds of ground beef.

He added a couple of diced onions and peppers. He added whatever spices he could find in the slide-out pantry and let the whole thing simmer.

In a slow-cooker that he always carried just for chili, he added several cans of diced tomatoes, crushed tomatoes and a couple of real tomatoes.

When the beef was brown enough, he drained the grease and added the frying pan contents to the tomatoes and stirred. After covering the slow cooker, he ventured into the bathroom for a shower.

He turned on the water. Nothing.

Checking the control panel, he discovered that he was completely out of fresh water, and his other tanks should be drained. Damn. He should have stopped and filled up with water somewhere and pumped out his tanks before he'd parked his rig here, but he was anxious to stop for the day after driving all night.

He had no other choice but to drive to the nearest pump facility. He'd pump out and fill up with water.

Dry camping was for the birds when he was with two females. Maybe he should have camped at one of the nearby campgrounds after all, but he didn't want to work out the logistics. Besides, he'd wanted his fellow riders and their families to meet his...daughter.

Yes. He considered Rose his daughter.

What did that make Lisa? She wasn't his sister-in-law anymore now that Rick and Carol were deceased.

She certainly wasn't his girlfriend.

At one time he would have shuddered at the thought, but now he just puzzled over the fact that he hadn't shuddered.

Go figure.

He went outside and told the camper next to them, his pal Jess Caruthers who was sitting outside with a cup of coffee, that he needed to pump out and that he'd be right back. He told Jess to let Lisa know.

He put the pot of chili into the sink, bracing it with old copies of *Pro Bull Rider Magazine* so it wouldn't slide around. Backing out carefully, he headed for the closest dump station, which was at a nearby RV dealership.

Traffic was heavy on the highway, and most of the time he barely moved. Eyeing the gas gauge, he decided to pull out of line and get some gas.

A lime-green VW bug followed him out of line and stayed close to his bumper. Sully didn't think anything of it until four women jumped out of the car at the gas station.

"Sully!" said a tall blonde with big hair. "I've been waiting to see you."

"Me, too!"

"And me!"

The shortest one eyed him up and down. "You're looking hot, Sully."

He felt hot. The Florida sun was blazing overhead.

They all had big hair and smelled of buckets of different perfume. They gathered around him, and the blonde slipped her hand into his.

"I'm going to need my hand back, miss, so I can pump gas," Sully said, not quite sure how to handle this situation.

"Can we see inside your RV?" the one with the shortest shorts asked.

"That's not a good idea," Sully said.

"Well, we think it's a great idea. We'll warm it up for you."

Sully slid his credit card into the slot and hit the button for the gas he wanted. "It's warm enough in there."

"Where's your girlfriend?"

"My what?"

"The woman with the blond hair and the attitude. Oh, and we met your little girl. She's really cute."

Sully scratched his head. "Where did you—"

"The skank said that you were busy. We didn't believe her."

"Lisa is not a skank," Sully said. He was about to say more, but his thoughts were interrupted.

"Is the little girl yours, Sully? Tell me. I have to know." The tall blonde sounded serious. She grabbed his hand again and held it to her breast. "I can be a good mother." He quickly pulled his hand out and pushed hers away.

This whole scene was making him uncomfortable. How old were these girls, anyway? Old enough to drive, but that still didn't make them legal. Alarms were going off in his head.

Thankfully, the gas pump clicked off. "Ladies, I have

to get going. See you tonight at the arena." He screwed the gas cap back on and closed the little door. He couldn't wait to get away and back to the quiet of his RV.

"Oh, Sully!" The blonde took him by surprise by wrapping her arms around his neck and planting a kiss squarely on his lips.

"Hey!" he protested. "Don't do that!"

"My name is Tiffany." She slipped a piece of paper into the front pocket of his cutoffs before he could stop her. "Call me for a good time."

"How old are you, Tiffany?" All he could think about was Rose. He'd better not catch her doing something like this no matter how old she was.

Tiffany pulled out her driver's license and handed it to him as if he were a bouncer at the door of the nearest honky-tonk.

Tiffany had just turned eighteen, if her ID was to be believed.

There might have been a time when he would have flirted with these women and met them for a drink or two. But now they seemed so young, and so immature.

Hell, they *were* young and immature.

Or maybe he'd grown up a bit and started checking IDs.

He tipped his hat to the buckle bunnies and went into the gas station for some water and a couple of candy bars.

When he went back to the RV, both the girls and the VW were gone. Good.

He hit the highway again, chewing on chocolate. Finally, he found the dump station, and he was out of there in record time. He got sidetracked when he saw a character store and decided to stop.

He'd love to buy some T-shirts for Rose.

With a big smile at his good fortune, he parked in an "RV Only" area near the store.

* * *

Lisa pulled the little red wagon loaded with washed and folded laundry. She sipped an icy blue drink that she'd bought at a convenience store. The Florida humidity was getting to her.

Although Leland's Laundromat advertised in the front window that it was air-conditioned, it was still hot in there. It was even hotter on the walk back.

She arrived back at the arena only to find that Sully's motor home was gone.

Looking around for some kind of message from him, all she found was an aluminum folding chair, which she promptly sat in.

The sun blazed overhead, and she wished she'd had a hat and some sunscreen.

Taking out a towel from the pile of laundry, she wiped her face with it, then draped it over her head like a veil.

She must look like a derelict.

Thank goodness she had the blue stuff to drink.

In the food tent, it seemed like lunch was in the preparation stages. Lisa's stomach growled, reminding her that it was nearing lunchtime. She was surprised because she'd had an unusually big breakfast. One that turned in her stomach when she had the flashback to her childhood communes.

"It's just a gathering of friends." Lisa repeated Sully's words like a mantra.

Speaking of Sully…where the hell was he?

Was he overwhelmed by the responsibility thrust upon him, so he decided that he'd had enough and simply took off?

No. Sully might be a lot of things, but he wouldn't leave her and Rose stranded. Well, maybe her, but certainly not Rose.

Suddenly, she felt uneasy for thinking that Sully would move out and for not trusting him.

She couldn't help it. She barely knew him.

If he did leave them stranded, there wouldn't be a rock that he could hide under. She'd hunt him down like the low-down vermin that he was.

How would they get home? Her purse was in the RV. She didn't have any money, any charge cards, her driver's license or her cell phone.

She'd have to swallow her pride and call her mother or father to send her money. The lawyer would find out, and Rose would be taken away from them, from her.

Lisa was working herself into quite a lather when she saw Rose walking with Lacy and her mother. Lisa waved and hurried to meet them.

When she walked Rose back to the empty RV spot, the little girl burst into tears.

"Where's Uncle Sully? Where's our motor home?"

"Sweetie, don't cry. Uncle Sully will be right back. He probably went to the store."

"For what?" Rose sniffed.

"Honey, I don't know. Maybe something that he needed for the chili he's making for lunch with the rest of the campers."

Lisa moved the lawn chair to a patch of shade and Rose climbed onto her lap. They both shared the pink towel as a cover over their heads. The little girl put her head on Lisa's chest and fell asleep.

Elaine Scoggins, wife of L. T. Scoggins, one of the top-five bull riders, approached them with a big beach umbrella.

She put an index finger over her lips, meaning that Lisa didn't have to say anything to her. It might wake up Rose. Elaine set up the umbrella and gave her two plastic bottles of water.

She blew Lisa a kiss, and Lisa blew one back to thank her for her kindness. It was so sweet of her that it brought tears to Lisa's eyes.

She was going to kill Sully, the thoughtless cowboy. He could have left her a note. Damn his miserable hide.

Just as she decided to wake up Rose and move with the shade, she saw Sully's motor home roll in. He waved to her, smiling hugely, as if he didn't have a care in the world. Of course he didn't. He was in an air-conditioned vehicle.

Lisa didn't know whether to be relieved that Sully came back or to rage at him.

She was hot and sweaty and cranky. Her fingers were sticky from her blue drink.

Sully pulled in and she could feel the hot blast of the RV's engine. He cut the motor and just as she was about to stand up, he hurried down the stairs and held out his arms to pick up Rose.

"She's out like a light," he said softly.

"And she's hot," Lisa snapped.

He looked at Lisa after he lifted Rose. "You look hot, too."

"No kidding. And that's not the only thing wrong with me." She shot him her best glare.

"Come into the RV. The air conditioning is on, and the ice cubes are plentiful."

Lisa went up the stairs first and held the door open for Sully because Rose was draped over his shoulder like a toga.

"Let's put her on the big bed," Sully said.

After Rose was settled into bed, Lisa was going to have it out with Sully.

She opened the door to the bedroom and stepped inside. Then she stopped, stupefied.

In the bed was the tall blonde she'd met earlier—the same one the security guards had escorted off the premises. Her back was against the faux leather headboard that was built into the wall. The sheet was just about falling off her bare breasts. She had to be naked.

Now she knew what Sully had been doing. Rocking the motor home!

"Sully, you need to relocate your guest immediately. And change the sheets," Lisa snapped. She turned to leave and collided into him.

"What?" he asked, eyebrows furrowed.

"You heard me." Lisa took Rose from his arms. She walked over to the passenger's seat and sat down, rubbing Rose's back. She turned to have a full view of what was happening in the doorway of the bedroom. If that…groupie didn't leave, then she and Rose would.

She wouldn't allow Sully to flaunt his buckle bunnies in front of their niece.

How dare he bring her into…uh…*their* home!

"Tiffany?" she heard him ask from the doorway. "What the hell are you doing in here?"

He knew her name but seemed surprised that she was in the bedroom. Where did he expect her to be, holed up in the bathroom?

She didn't hear Tiffany's answer, but then Sully said, "Get dressed and get out."

Not exactly love talk from Mr. Good Time Sully.

Lisa heard a sing-song whine from Tiffany, but she couldn't make out her words.

"Yeah," Sully said. "Yeah, Lisa's my girlfriend. The little girl is Rose. She's ours. That's why you have to go, Tiffany. Get dressed. Show's over."

Whoa! What did he say?

I'm so not his girlfriend!

He closed the door, probably to give Tiffany some privacy. Lisa was surprised he did that, thinking that Sully wouldn't want to miss seeing the blonde naked again.

For a good-time cowboy, he was showing remarkable restraint.

Lisa still didn't like him bringing his "dates" back to the motor home, and she was going to tell him so in very clear terms.

Sully couldn't believe that this woman was in his motor home and in his bed.

He thought back. She must have snuck in while he was at the convenience store. The VW had gone, but Tiffany had stayed.

If he had known, he would have kicked her ass out. Thank goodness Rose was asleep and didn't witness Tiffany naked in his bed.

Tiffany finally opened the door to the bedroom. She was fully clothed, her hair was fluffed and she was drenched in perfume.

"Tiffany, don't do this again, please," he said.

"But, Sully—"

He held up a hand like a traffic cop. "I told you that I have a girlfriend and a child."

He pointed to Lisa and Rose sitting in the passenger's seat. Lisa must have heard him calling her his girlfriend because she raised her hand in a wave.

Rose was draped over Lisa. The poor kid was tired and should be in bed by now. Instead, he'd had to deal with Tiffany.

"But, Sully, I told you before that your bio on the PBR website doesn't mention that you have a girlfriend and a kid. I'm no home wrecker."

So Tiffany had scruples.

"Tiffany, what would your parents say if they found

out that you snuck into my bed?" Sully asked. Damn, he sounded like an old man!

She rolled her eyes. "I do what I want. I'm old enough."

Sully was just about to lecture her on safe sex, but he decided that it wasn't his place.

"I'll update the PBR website. Until then, goodbye, Tiffany. Find another cowboy."

He held the door open for her. He didn't particularly like the fact that everyone would see her exit his rig. It just didn't look right.

She tossed her blond hair and walked down the three steps. Sully glanced around. Everyone was gathering for the late lunch, so no one was nearby. That was a break.

Closing the door, he walked into the bedroom, pulled off the linens and tossed them into the bathroom. The laundry bag was gone because Lisa hadn't had a chance to unload her red wagon.

Lisa. He was dreading the confrontation with her. She looked really mad. He half expected her to paw the dirt like an angry bull.

He hurried to make the bed again.

When he was done, he waved to Lisa to bring Rose.

Lisa struggled to get up. Then she shook her head. He hurried to the front of the RV.

"My legs are numb," Lisa explained.

Gently, he took Rose from her. The little girl moaned slightly and snuggled against him. He walked to the bedroom and tucked her into the fresh sheets.

Rose was out cold. Other than to burrow into the pillow, she barely moved.

Now it was time for him to explain things to Lisa before she imploded.

He walked to the front of the RV. Lisa hadn't moved from

the passenger's seat. "I didn't know she was in the RV," Sully said, jumping right in.

"Who are you kidding?"

"You don't believe me?"

"You left us stranded in the parking lot, Sully. Why? So you could pick up Tiffany and rock the RV?"

"What are you talking about? I took the RV to the pumping station. We didn't have a drop of water left."

"You took it where?"

"To the pumping station at the Sunrise Palms RV dealership."

She put her hands on her hips and her jaw fell open. She shook her head. "And how was I supposed to know that, Sully? You could have left me a message."

"I did. I told Jess Caruthers to tell you."

"Well, he didn't."

"He must have gone to the arena. Or maybe he's at the gym."

Lisa shrugged. "You could have left me a note."

"Where? On the tar?"

"On the lawn chair you left behind. The same chair that Rose and I sat on with a towel over our heads because we were melting in the ninety-degree heat."

"I am totally sorry about that. But, Lisa, we didn't have a drop of water. I thought I'd be back before you, but the traffic was heavy."

"You could have called me on my cell phone!"

"That one?" He pointed to her cell phone, which she'd left in the beverage holder on the console of the RV.

She closed her eyes. "Yeah, that one. But what about Tiffany?" she asked. "Why, Sully?"

"It's not what you think. I stopped at a gas station to fill up. Tiffany was there with her girlfriends. They followed me. While I was in the convenience store, Tiffany must have slipped inside. That's all there is to that story."

Lisa was silent. Obviously she didn't believe him.

"Look, I'd never bring anyone back to the RV, especially with Rose here. Tiffany is a total buckle bunny. She thinks that she's in love with me, but she isn't. She's just young."

"That was quite the lecture you gave her."

"Yeah. I didn't know where that came from. I felt like an old man."

"You sounded mature."

Sully laughed. "Don't tell anyone. It'll ruin my reputation."

Lisa finally cracked a smile.

He held out a hand. "Are we good? Do you trust me to do what's best for Rose?"

She looked at his hand, gave a big sigh, then clasped his. They shook.

"Yeah, we're good, but the next time, call me on my cell, will you? And I'll be sure to take it with me. Or leave a note."

"You could try to trust me, you know," Sully said.

"That might be a little harder."

"Why?"

"Your reputation precedes you."

"Try and forget about my reputation," he said.

Sully knew that'd be impossible for Lisa to do. She had already judged him and labeled him a party animal. He liked a good party as much as the next guy, but now he had major responsibilities. He had to take that into consideration.

"Are you hungry?" he asked Lisa, checking his chili.

Lisa took a big sniff of the air.

"Smells good, Sully."

"It really does smell good," Sully said, handing her a spoon that he'd dipped into the chili.

Lisa blew on the hot chili, and then tasted it. "Sully, it's delicious. What's your secret?"

Sully grinned. "My special blend of herbs is my secret, which just means that I toss in whatever's on hand. Then I drive it around Florida for a while and take it to the Sunshine Palms RV dealership. Then turn it down low while I take a shower at the Surfer's Paradise bathhouse for seventy-five cents."

She chuckled and handed the spoon back to him. "You know, Sully, I believe you."

"About the Sunshine Palms, the bathhouse or my chili recipe?"

"About Tiffany."

They were back to that. "It's kind of funny if you think about it," he said.

She rolled her eyes and pouffed up her hair like Tiffany.

"'Sully, you'd better update the PBR website. I'm not a home wrecker.'" Lisa mimicked the girl in a falsetto voice.

"What are we going to do if one of us actually has a date?" Sully asked.

Lisa shrugged. "I don't want a parade of faux aunts and uncles coming and going in Rose's life. It'd be too much for her."

"I agree. So what do we do?"

"Maybe we shouldn't bring any of them home."

He thought for a while. "Yeah. You're probably right. It's better that we sneak around."

"That's not what I meant."

"I know what you meant," he said.

That'd be an interesting dilemma. Dating.

"I guess there's always a hotel room," she said.

He looked at Lisa. Her dark green eyes were twinkling. She was thinking all this was hilarious.

"You know, Sully, I don't know how long you can remain

celibate, but I think that Rose should be our first priority. We should put our sexual needs aside."

"Celibate?" He laughed. "Are you kidding?"

Chapter Eight

Sully finally stopped laughing enough to concentrate on his chili.

Yeah, she was kidding. She didn't expect any healthy, red-blooded male, such as Sully, to say no to sex if the occasion presented itself.

Lisa couldn't remember the last time she'd had sex. She'd been too busy to develop a relationship with a guy, and she wasn't the type for one-night stands.

She'd had several opportunities for casual sex with other pilots and a couple of Atlanta air traffic controllers over the past couple of years, but she'd passed.

She had to feel something for a man with her heart before she gave him her body.

That was about the only thing she learned from the communes she'd grown up in. They weren't the "free sex" type, thank goodness, and they stressed family life and commitment to one spouse. They even stressed marriage in some form, either a formal ceremony in the church or just a gathering outdoors with the other members of the commune.

Marriage. Carol couldn't wait to get married, and she was lucky that she'd found Rick in college. They were made for each other. They'd gotten married at St. Margaret's Church in Palm Springs to appease Rick's parents and then got married again at the commune's flower garden to appease hers.

The reception at the Lakeshore Yacht and Country Club couldn't have been more exquisite, including a chamber orchestra and a six-course dinner.

The party at the commune had been a picnic on blankets with someone strumming the guitar and a lot of women drumming.

Okay, okay, Lisa had to admit that she liked to drum.

She sighed. She couldn't picture herself getting married like her sister. She couldn't imagine wanting to be with someone for the rest of her life. She was too picky, too fussy, too compulsive.

And she was too scared to share her life, her thoughts, her soul with anyone.

"I'm going to take this over to the lunch," Sully said. His hands were covered in oven gloves in the shape of bulls, complete with ears, and he held his crock of chili at waist level. "I'll grab a plate, then come back and eat here so I can listen for Rose. Then you can go and eat."

Lisa nodded. "Sounds like a plan." She held the door open for Sully. The red wagon heaped with clothes caught her eye. In the Tiffany confusion, she'd forgotten to put the clothes away.

She walked down the steps and reached for a stack.

Sully put the chili down. "I'll hand them to you."

"No. Go. You have to eat and get to the arena. I can take care of the clothes. Oh, and I can take care of letting Molly out to do her business. And cleaning Snowball's litter pan."

"Lisa Phillips, you are a good egg."

Off he went, whistling.

"Oh yeah, I'm a good egg," she mumbled sarcastically.

She stood there in front of the wagon watching him go. He had a spring in his step, and he could really work a pair of jeans.

He looked every bit the cowboy: hat, boots, long-sleeved, Western-cut shirt, clean shaven and a shiny belt buckle the size of Montana.

Lisa didn't know why she was ogling him as he walked toward the food tent. She supposed that she liked the way he walked or the way his boots sounded on the asphalt. Maybe both.

Just then he turned and looked at her. Grinning, he winked.

Oh, no! Busted!

Embarrassment heated her cheeks. Why did that always happen? She quickly picked up more clothes from the red wagon. Maybe he'd think that she was just looking at something else if she didn't respond.

She didn't want Sully to think that she was the slightest bit interested in him.

But she was.

Maybe *interested* wasn't the right word. Bewildered, confused, perplexed—that was what she'd been feeling about Sully ever since he'd held her hand in Carol's garden.

Could she have been misjudging him all these years? He hadn't been with Tiffany as she'd assumed, and she liked the way he'd kicked her out. His thoughts were about Rose, and she liked that. Maybe he wasn't the womanizing cowboy that she'd thought.

No. He probably still was the same womanizing cowboy, but at least he was thinking about Rose now. That was the only difference.

Lisa wasn't going to cut him any slack. She had formed an opinion of him based on her interaction with him over the years, and it would take a lot of change on Sully's part to revise her opinion of him.

She put away the laundry, tiptoeing into the bedroom to access the drawers and closet space. Rose was still sleeping soundly. Good. They had a big night planned. Rose couldn't wait to see her uncle ride a big bull in person.

Sully returned to the RV just as Lisa sat down at the dinette with a can of iced tea and the mug of chili he'd left her.

It was still warm, and it was delicious. She'd have to get Sully to show her how to make it step-by-step.

Sully slid two heaped paper plates onto the dinette table. "I thought I'd save you a trip to the buffet in this heat. Hope you like what I picked out for you."

Lisa looked at the ham and cheese sandwich, the potato salad, the fried chicken and the plastic cup with what looked like chocolate pudding. Maybe she'd put the sandwich in a bag and save it for later.

"Everything is perfectly fine, Sully. Thanks. And your chili is delicious."

He nodded. "Several of the ladies said that they are looking forward to seeing you again. They wondered if you were sick. I told them that you were under the weather."

"That was presumptuous of you, Sully. I'm not under the weather. I just did laundry and then walked with my little red wagon in this heat and—" She waved her hand. No sense rehashing the whole miscommunication. "I'm just…tired."

"I hear you and raise you."

Now she noticed the bags under his eyes and the stoop to his shoulders. After driving all night, finding the pump station, making chili and dealing with Tiffany, he must be exhausted.

He'd only had about a couple of hours of sleep, and that wasn't enough to be in top-notch shape.

Lisa checked her watch. In a few hours, he had to ride a two-thousand-pound bucking bull for eight seconds (hopefully), get off, get his bearings and then run to safety before the wild animal charged at him.

Just another day in Brett Sullivan's world.

No. It was her world, too, now.

And Rose's.

Sully smiled and waved to the bunch of giggling buckle bunnies—including Tiffany—who were gathered near the contestant's entrance at the arena. He noticed that Tiffany had set her sights on T. J. Gibbs, one of the up-and-coming young guns. T.J. was autographing her midriff, but Tiffany's eyes were already looking around for a bigger star.

Sully settled his gear bag higher onto his shoulder and took the elevator down to the sub-basement. When the big silver doors opened, the pungent smell of earth and bull manure assailed his senses.

Waving to his fellow riders, he checked the day sheet for his first ride: Cowabunga, one of the rankest bulls bucking these days and a contender for Bull of the Year. Swearing under his breath, he knew that he had to be at the top of his game to go eight seconds on him.

But he wasn't at the top of his game. He was tired and unprepared.

Normally, he'd hit a friend's ranch and ride some practice bulls, analyze his previous rides for improvement and study the rides of the top guns. He'd hit the gym, then hit the track to do some sprints and his customized sequences of yoga stretches.

He'd done nothing.

He didn't even get a good night's sleep.

That was his fault. He was the one who decided to pull an all-nighter. He really should have taken Lisa up on her offer to drive, but he'd rather that she care for Rose's needs.

Maybe if his little niece was a Russ or a Ross, he could handle things better, but then she wouldn't be his little niece.

Sully liked to take a walk around the arena before the event got started. He like to watch the arena commentators getting ready, the dirt being raked, the eight-second clock being checked for accuracy. He gave a wave to the day sheet salesman, tipped his hat to the fan club volunteers who'd be selling memberships and merchandise later and had a conversation with the stock contractor of Cowabunga, his first draw.

And he watched the fans file in and take their seats.

Needing to see Lisa and Rose, he walked back to the bucking chutes and climbed up the metal stairs behind them.

They weren't in their seats yet.

Looking up, he checked the arena clock. There was a lot of time left, so he really was surprised not to see them seated yet. He leaned against the metal railing, visualizing his ride. The stock contractor said that Cowabunga would go left, so Sully figured that he'd go right.

Never can trust those stock contractors.

Sully figured that he had chewed up about fifteen minutes, but when he checked the clock again, only five minutes had passed. He felt like Lisa, who always checked her watch.

He felt jittery, unsettled. He couldn't wait until it was time for him to ride, but until then, he'd better get ready.

He took one last look at the section where friends and family would sit.

Damn. The biggest player in the history of bull riding, Chase Gatlin, was helping Lisa and Rose to their seats. Chase had a grin as big as Texas, and no doubt the cowboy was heaping on the charisma.

He had his hand on the small of Lisa's back, and—hey!—
he just picked up Rose! Rose took his hat off and put it on
her own head. She was giggling and Chase was tickling her.

Sully found himself grinding his teeth. What the hell was
Chase doing? What was Lisa doing with him?

Lisa was too smart to fall for Chase's over-the-top drawl
and the dropping of every g at the end of every verb phrase.
Some women liked that kind of thing, but Lisa would never
fall for Chase's act.

Watching her, you'd never know it.

And what was she wearing?

The Wranglers he'd bought her fit her like a second skin.
She wore a light blue long-sleeved shirt, which she'd tucked
into the waistband of her jeans. She even sported a big silver belt buckle and a white cowboy hat.

Those were his hat, his shirt, his belt buckle…they were
all his!

Sully had to chuckle, thinking what Chase Gatlin would
say to the fact that the object of Chase's lust, for the moment, was wearing Sully's stuff.

Sully had no intention of spilling Lisa's secret, even if
it wasn't a secret. As a matter of fact, he liked the idea that
she'd wanted to dress Western tonight in the Wranglers that
he'd bought her instead of her expensive designer duds.

Maybe there was hope for the Ice Queen yet.

He checked the arena clock again. Time to get ready.
Making his way down the chutes and down the stairs, he
gave one last look at the family and friends section. He saw
Chase making his way out of the stands.

Rose was on Lisa's lap, and they were looking around.
When Lisa spotted him, she smiled and waved, sending a
warm feeling through him.

Then Lisa showed Rose where he was standing.

"Uncle Sully!" Rose shouted, rising to her feet. "There's

Uncle Sully." Her tiny voice echoed through the mostly empty arena as clear as a bell in winter. Several people laughed and clapped.

Sully jogged across the arena, climbed up the fence and the metal barricade that protected the spectators from the bulls, then climbed up the rows that led to Lisa and Rose.

He tipped his hat. "Hello, ladies!"

"Uncle Sully!" Rose held her arms out to be picked up, and he did so. "Be careful of the bulls. They can hurt you."

Aww…how cute.

"I will, sweetheart. I'll be careful. You just cheer and clap for me, okay? It'll bring me luck."

He turned to Lisa and nodded. "You're looking good, Lisa. Just like a real cowgirl."

"A real cowgirl, huh?" She winked. Was she flirting?

He looked her up and down and liked what he saw.

"You sure do."

He handed Rose back, and the girl settled onto Lisa's lap again.

"Good luck tonight, Sully." She held up her day sheet. "Ride Cowabunga for eight. You can do it. He'll go right in the chutes, then he'll immediately turn back left."

He held up a thumb. "Okay. Got it." He got a kick out of the fact that Lisa watched bull riding on TV. He liked to think that she watched it for him, but he knew better.

He was climbing back down the seats when Lisa shouted. "Sully?"

He stopped. "Yeah?"

"Please be careful."

He pushed his hat back with a thumb to make sure he was talking to the correct woman. There was a time that she'd wished him maybe not dead, or maimed or injured, but at least two thousand miles away from her.

CHRISTINE WENGER   103

She cupped her hands and put them over Rose's ears. "I don't want Rose to see anything bad happen to you."

"Lisa, should that happen, I'd like you to have my personal effects," he said as solemnly as he could muster.

She pointed to Rose, then put an index finger over her lips. "Shh...Sully!"

"That would be my motor home, my gear bag and the clothes you are wearing."

"Oh, for... Sully, you... Just go, will you, please?"

He had the urge, a primal urge, to pull Lisa into his arms and lay a big kiss on her lips.

He couldn't believe that he was thinking of kissing the Ice Queen, Lisa Phillips. He had to be sleep-deprived or just plain crazy. Knowing how negatively his kiss would be received, he turned and hurried to the locker room.

No matter how great she looked tonight or how much he enjoyed teasing her, Lisa Phillips just wasn't for him.

He couldn't believe he was even thinking along that line.

"Get your head on straight, cowboy," he mumbled to himself as he slid his chaps on. "You have a rank bull to ride, an event to win and a three-year-old watching you who thinks that you can rope the moon."

Lisa couldn't wait until that arrogant cowboy Chase Gatlin left her and Rose alone.

Rose liked him enough, but if Chase had called her darlin' one more time, she was going to scream into her cowboy hat. Make that Sully's cowboy hat.

She smiled, thinking of how she'd slipped into Sully's shirt, a crisply pressed, blue-checked snap-up with long sleeves. It had been hanging in the closet of the motor home still in the clear dry cleaning bag.

She loved the belt with the silver conchos on it, but it needed something—a huge buckle. That's what everyone wore, a buckle the size of a platter. She found just what she needed hanging in the closet—a big belt buckle that said "Pueblo Invitational, Champion." She borrowed it and put it on her belt.

She smiled when she'd put on the boots that Sully bought her. She loved the green saguaros on the sides, the howling wolf and the full moon. If only her coworkers could see her now! They wouldn't believe it was her.

She loved how the boots clicked on the floor when she walked and how she almost felt…Western. It was like she was changing her persona for a while.

She had gotten Rose dressed, and then they were ready to go. Rose had been so excited to get there that she jumped and skipped as they walked.

They ran into Chase Gatlin near the will-call window when she went to pick up the tickets Sully had left for them. Lisa recognized Chase from TV and pegged him as a player a long time ago, so she was amused—and flattered—that he was trying to flirt with her.

Chase acted like it was his personal mission to show them their seats and make them comfortable, and Lisa continued to go along with him because he'd made Rose laugh. Besides, he had to leave soon to get ready to ride.

But it was Sully that she had been looking for, and when he had run across the arena dirt and climbed over the barricades to see them…well, she had to admit that made her heart race.

She'd loved when he kidded her about the clothes, and she couldn't believe that he joked about his will, but no matter, he always made her laugh.

The national anthem started and they all stood. Then the riders were introduced with a hail of fireworks and smoke, followed by the Cowboy Prayer.

Soon the first rider was bucking off.

And although Rose was fascinated to see the big bulls up close and personal, she couldn't wait to see Uncle Sully. Sully was the twelfth rider.

And finally, he was up. Rose yelled and waved. Lisa held her breath.

Eight seconds seemed to go on forever. Cowabunga did go right first, just as Lisa predicted. She hoped that Sully was paying attention. Cowabunga did everything but pull a gun on Sully to get the cowboy off his back, but Sully stuck like burdock.

The seconds ticked by.

Finally, the buzzer rang. Sully had done it! He had ridden the rankest bull in the pen.

Now all he had to do was get away.

Sully fell sideways off the bull. Two of the bull fighters tried to divert Cowabunga, but the bull had a different idea.

He wanted Sully.

Cowabunga charged. Three of the bull fighters couldn't divert the bull and found themselves on the arena dirt.

Sully tried to outrun the animal, but he didn't have a chance. Cowabunga bent his head and tossed Sully up in the air with his horns.

Sully hit the dirt and the bull stepped around him, after stepping on Sully's foot twice.

Lisa's mouth wet dry. "Get the bull out of the arena!" she yelled to the rider with miles of rope in his hand. "Rope him!"

Thank goodness, the bull left the arena and went back through the open gate that led to the bull pens behind the chutes.

"Why doesn't Uncle Sully get up?" Rose asked.

Lisa was so caught up in worrying about Sully, she hadn't given a thought to Rose.

What kind of guardian was she?

"Uncle Sully seems to have twisted his ankle or something," Lisa replied. "He'll be fine. The doctor is looking at him."

Rose's bottom lip quivered, and Lisa hugged the girl to her. Maybe she shouldn't have brought her, but after watching it on TV, Rose knew exactly what to expect; she just didn't expect that Uncle Sully would be one of the cowboys who'd get hurt.

Finally, Sully was on his feet and waving to the crowd. Sports medicine staff were supporting him, but he was at least upright. Rose cheered, and Lisa finally breathed.

She couldn't believe how much she'd worried about him.

The arena announcers stated that Sully's ankle wasn't broken, but it was badly bruised and that he'd be back to ride again in the short round.

Then Sully limped to where they were sitting, removed his hat and waved it to her and Rose. Then he blew a kiss—obviously to Rose.

Rose clapped her hands and jumped around.

The arena announcer wondered out loud who Sully was greeting. The camera panned to them just as Lisa was showing Rose how to blow a kiss back.

But the camera didn't show that part. It just showed Sully and Lisa blowing kisses to each other.

The arena announcer and the entertainer bull fighter took the opportunity to make a big deal out of it. They made Sully seem like a lovesick cowboy, but she fared much better. She was the "mysterious hottie" who had captured the heart of one of the top bull riders.

Hottie? Her?

This was her fifteen minutes of fame? If so, she'd take a pass. She didn't want to be known as anyone's hottie, least of all Brett Sullivan's.

She held her breath, waiting for it to all go away and for them to move on to the next thing.

Luckily, she didn't have too long to wait. It was soon announced that Sully was advised by the sports medicine staff not to ride in the short go. They wanted him to get an X-ray on his foot.

Sully said that he was going to ride anyway.

Darn that stubborn man.

Was winning that important that Sully would risk his health? Why wasn't he thinking of her and Rose?

Lisa sighed. He was thinking of them. He was thinking of winning and bringing in some money. He was thinking of accumulating enough points for the World Finals.

And all she could think of was how she didn't want him to be hurt anymore.

Chapter Nine

It was time for Sully to ride again, and Lisa was getting adept at holding her breath. He had drawn Bongo, a young bull who was noted for spinning.

If Sully could stay on, he'd probably earn more than ninety points.

The sound of metal crashing against metal filled the arena as the gate opened. The bull went right, then left, then right again, and Sully managed to stay on. Then the bull started to spin.

It looked like Sully was going to fall off, and Lisa screamed, "Ride him, Sully. Ride him!"

Rose echoed, "Ride him!" with her little hands cupped over her mouth.

Lisa took her niece's hand, and they both yelled. Eight seconds seemed like eight weeks as finally the horn blew.

"He did it, Rose! He did it!"

"He did it," she agreed.

It took forever for his score to come in. "Ninety-two points," yelled the arena announcer.

The place erupted in cheers, and Rose put her hands over her ears.

"Meet the winner of the Fort Lauderdale Invitational, Brett 'Sully' Sullivan!" the announcer said.

Sully's interview could be heard over the loudspeaker. Cameras flashed and Sully was presented with a gold belt buckle and a fishing rod and reel.

"I'd like to thank the two ladies in my life, Lisa and Rose," Sully said. "And my sponsors."

While Sully listed his sponsors, most of the crowd moved to the exits. Lisa wanted to shout at them all to be quiet and listen to Sully's speech.

When the presentation was over, she and Rose shuffled along with the crowd. She could hear several people talking about how Sully seemed to have a new energy about him and a new commitment to winning and winning big.

They attributed it all to the mystery woman in his life and the little girl. A few close friends knew that Rose was his niece and that Lisa was his sister-in-law and, due to unfortunate circumstances, the two of them were Rose's guardians. Most people didn't know the circumstances, though.

Whatever the reason for his sudden motivation, Sully was hot, and he needed to keep riding to keep his stats up.

"Lisa, open the door!" said a man with a baritone voice.

Lisa opened the door of the motor home as wide as possible and three bull riders carried Sully in.

"Where do you want him?" Chase Gatlin asked.

"The dinette will be fine," she said.

"The what?" another cowboy grunted.

"The kitchen booth," Lisa clarified.

"Oh."

They hoisted him into the booth, and Sully stretched out his leg. "Thanks for the lift, guys."

No one, least of all Lisa, would have known that the man before her with scrapes, bruises and an ankle packed in ice was currently the top bull rider in the world.

He looked more like a prize fighter who'd lost his match—and lost badly.

"No problem, Sully," said Chase, eyeing Lisa appreciatively. He winked. "I was lookin' for you and Rose after the event."

"Rose was tired. We came right back here so I could put her to bed."

"Well, darlin'." Chase tipped his hat. "Maybe some other time we could hit a honky-tonk and do some boot scootin' and—"

"Thanks again for your help, Chase," Sully interrupted. "And, just so you know, Lisa is with me."

Lisa raised her eyebrow but didn't say anything. She could take care of Chase Gatlin herself, but quite frankly she was enjoying the attention from the cowboy—both cowboys. It had been a while since she'd felt...desirable.

But was that a hint of jealousy she detected coming from Sully? To think that Sully would be jealous of Chase was laughable; nonetheless, Sully had made it known that they were...together.

She wasn't kidding herself. Sully just wanted to let Chase know that she was off-limits because of Rose. Well, she didn't intend on being a hermit or celibate any more than Sully did if the right opportunity presented itself.

"Good night, Chase." Lisa took him by the arm to lead him to the door. "Thanks for everything that you did for Sully."

"Are you really with him, darlin'?" Chase whispered.

She nodded. "We're going to be together for a while,

Chase. I'm going to have to take a rain check on that honky-tonk thing."

"That's too bad." He blatantly stared at her, his gaze lingering on her breasts.

She opened the door and just about tossed him down the stairs. Quickly, she closed and locked the door, then slid into the other seat of the dinette.

"How are you doing, Sully?"

He inhaled deeply and exhaled. "I've been worse. This is nothing."

Silence.

"What do we do now?" Lisa asked.

"We?"

"Yes. We."

"Help me out here, Lisa. What are you going for?" Sully asked.

"Rose's heart will be broken if we don't take her to Disney World."

"Then we should go," Sully said. "We're close enough."

"But look at you, Sully. They had to cut your boot off."

He shrugged. "It was an old boot."

She had to laugh. "That's not what I meant." She took a deep breath. "What if you'd really gotten hurt? What if—"

"Injury is a given in my line of work. It's not *if* I'll get hurt, it's *when*."

She bit her bottom lip. She didn't know if she could live like that. "I am counting on you to help me with Rose. If you are injured, you can't help. And then I'll end up having to take care of you, too."

Sully's jaw dropped. "I've never thought about that," he said quietly. "I'll hire a nurse if I need one. You won't have to do a thing."

"Oh, Sully, that's not my point."

"What is your point?"

"That you're in a dangerous profession. If something should happen to you, it'd be just me and Rose."

He took his hat off and grinned. "I'm glad you have confidence in my ability to ride."

"You're a good rider, but things can happen. You said so yourself."

"Lisa, if something should happen to me, you'll do fine with Rose alone, but nothing is going to happen to me."

"Promise?"

"Promise. And I'll change my will. You'll be well-protected."

"Oh most definitely, Sully. I'll take good care of your motor home." She grinned.

"And my real estate holdings and my bank account. That all totals a couple of million."

"A couple of what?" Her mouth hung open like a fish's.

"Yup." He grinned. "It's mostly my winnings since I started riding with the PBR. I don't spend a lot of money. I don't have a lot of needs. But enough about this depressing stuff."

"Um…just one more question, if you don't mind."

"Lay it on me," Sully said. "My life is an open book."

"You're a rich and successful bull rider, so why do your parents, particularly your father, put you down?"

"I've never told my father what I'm worth." He shook his head. "But being a cowboy is not what my parents consider a normal job. Rick had a 'normal' job. He sat at a desk and made money that way. He didn't have to travel, he didn't ride smelly animals and he didn't get dirty. Rick had a job that a father could be proud of. I am a cowboy and that's one step lower than a convict in his book."

"I get it now, but has he ever seen you ride?"

"Not to my knowledge."

Lisa shook her head. "What a shame."

"Thanks. That was nice of you to say."

Feeling uncomfortable with his compliment, she changed the subject. "How do we get you around? In a wheelchair?"

"Yup. But I'll rent one of those electric ones so no one has to push me," he said. "Maybe we'll get into some of the shows quicker."

She rolled her eyes. "You always find a silver lining, Sully. That's what I like about you."

"At least you like something about me."

"I like a lot of things about you," she said quickly.

"Like what?" He grinned. "Tell me."

"There's so much, Sully," she said sarcastically. "I don't have enough time to tell you everything. To change the subject, let me just ask you this—who is going to drive your motor home? You can't drive, and neither can Rose."

"Uh…that leaves you," he said. "I figure if you can drive jumbo jets, you can drive this rig."

"Piece of cake. We leave tomorrow morning after breakfast. Oh-eight-hundred hours."

"Let's leave at oh-eight-hundred hours and three minutes, just so we're not being rigid."

She grinned. "I'll get you a pillow and a blanket, Sully. You get the dinette. I'll sleep with Rose."

"Sounds like a plan."

She went to the closet and grabbed two blankets and a pillow. When she returned, Sully was already nodding off.

"I'll change the dinette into a bed, but you're going to have to get up," she said.

"I gotta freshen my ice pack anyway. Do we have more? This thing is throbbing."

"We do. I'll get it."

"I can get it." Sully tried to get out of the dinette booth by moving back and forth on his rear. "I see what you mean about having to take care of me, but don't. I can do it my-self."

"Sports medicine disagrees, Sully, so let me help you."

She took his hands and was able to pull him out of the dinette. However, when he stood, he looked like he was about to collapse. Lisa ducked under his arm and held him around the waist. "I've got you."

"Let's go over to the passenger's seat."

"That's just where I was headed. There's not a lot of seating options in here, you know."

He chuckled and let her help him. Sitting down, he took the ice pack from around his foot.

"I'll take care of that," Lisa said.

"Thanks."

She filled the bag with ice then returned to Sully. Bending over, she put the new pack in place.

"Thanks again, Lisa."

She nodded, then walked back over to the dinette. Like an RV pro, she unhooked the table, hooked it again on the lower wall bracket, then put the cushions in place. Shaking out the linens and blankets, she made the bed.

"Might be a little too short for you," she said.

"It'll be fine."

Nothing seemed to faze Sully. He was very easygoing and he didn't complain.

"Okay," she said. "You're all set. What else do you need?"

"Well…"

"Yes?"

"I hate to ask this, but do you think you can help me get my jeans off?"

She tried to remain cool, but her face began to heat. She'd seen her share of men without their jeans on or anything else, so why did the thought of helping Sully get undressed send her into a tailspin?

"No problem," she said with more confidence than she felt.

"I have a pair of shorts I can put on, just in case Rose wakes up. They're in the bedroom, top drawer, navy blue."

"Okay."

Her brief escape into the bedroom gave her some time to be alone, to catch her breath, to figure out why Brett Sullivan was making her crazy.

Sully didn't need as much help as he'd indicated to Lisa. He could have cut his jeans to get them over his swollen ankle, but he liked this pair and wanted to save them. With Lisa's help, he'd be able to get them off.

He had to admit that he liked watching the blush that crept up her cheeks when he'd asked her to help him. Fascinating. You'd think that such a woman of the world Lisa wouldn't feel embarrassed about much of anything.

He heard the door close quietly, and Lisa returned with his navy blue jogging shorts in her hands.

"How's Rose?"

"Out like a light. She had such a great time, Sully, and when you won, it was just perfect." Lisa tossed him the shorts, and he caught them with one hand. "No, I take that back. It was perfect when you blew her a kiss. You made her feel special."

"She is special."

"Definitely," Lisa agreed. "But she was asking about her mommy and daddy again. When she's overtired, she cries for them." Lisa stared at some place above his head. He knew she was thinking of her sister.

Sully felt every ache and pain from tonight's bull riding. He wished he could think of some magic words that could take away Rose's and Lisa's pain. All of their pain.

He thought about how Rose's little face lit up when he blew her that kiss, and that made him feel better.

Suddenly, Sully felt exhausted. Without thinking, he stood up, popped the button of his jeans and lowered his zipper. But then he almost fell sideways.

"Hang on, Sully. You're a little wobbly. And I have to take the ice pack off again."

"Okay."

She knelt on one knee, her gaze avoiding anything but the ice. "Can you lower your jeans some more and sit back down?"

He didn't think he could play this game any longer. Soon, he'd be showing more than he ever dreamed of in his tidy whities. He sat down.

"Uh...I can take it from here, Lisa."

"No. I'll help. Lift your legs."

She gripped the jeans and tugged gently. Slowly, his jeans slid down his legs and pooled at his ankles.

Carefully, she freed his bad ankle.

"Wow, is that swollen!" she exclaimed.

If she only knew...

"It's purple, Sully. Purple!"

Oh, damn.

He held his breath, hoping this would end soon.

His other ankle was freed, his socks were off and he was sitting in the passenger's seat in his underwear.

So far, Lisa had avoided looking above his knees. That changed when she held her hand out. He took her hand and covered it with both of his.

"I...um...just wanted you to hand me your shorts. I was going to help you into them," she said.

"Oh, sorry," he said, but he made no move to drop her hand. He just wanted to hold it for a while.

She looked at their clasped hands and raised an eyebrow. "What's up, Sully?"

"I want to thank you for everything you've done so far."

"Back atcha," she quipped.

"I'm serious, Lisa."

Her eyes finally met his. "Okay."

"We haven't had a fight in…how long?"

"Shall we count when you left us stranded here and the Tiffany debacle?"

"Okay, so it hasn't been that long," he said. Then he winked at her.

"Don't wink at me! It reminds me of Chase Gatlin."

"Hey, you don't like him, do you?" he asked.

"I think he'd be fun to go out boot scootin' with, as he says, but that's it."

It seemed like the most natural thing in the world, sitting there in his underwear and talking to Lisa.

"We really should set some rules for dating," he said. "I don't want a lot of men coming and going in Rose's life."

"I wasn't the one who drove Tiffany around the state of Florida."

"I only drove her around Fort Lauderdale."

"Oh, I beg your pardon," Lisa said.

He slipped his shorts over his ankles, stood and snapped the elastic waistband into place.

Lisa rolled her eyes. Had she figured out that he was semi-faking?

"Sully, what exactly is our relationship?" she asked.

"What do you mean?"

"What are we to each other?" Lisa asked.

"I don't know exactly what you're going for, but I guess we are friends working toward a common goal—the care of Rose."

"I think you summed it up perfectly."

"I did?"

"You did. We are friends. That's it. Friends. No more, no less."

"And your point is?"

"Whatever this charade was with me helping you with your jeans, don't even think of tricking me like that again."

"Tricking you?"

"Come on, Sully. You didn't need my help."

"Hey, I didn't know that. Not at first."

She grunted. "You could have called it off."

"I could have."

"Why didn't you?" she asked.

"I was enjoying myself and enjoying watching you."

"Isn't that mature of you?"

"Hey, I never said that I was mature."

"Friends," she said. "We are just friends, and that's all we're ever going to be. Good night, Sully."

Before he could say anything, she was gone.

Chapter Ten

Brett Sullivan is incorrigible, Lisa thought as she lay in bed listening to the soft rise and fall of Rose's breathing. The little girl had snuggled up to her side, and Lisa put her arm around her niece.

Molly and Snowball were present, too. Molly was stretched out at the foot of the bed. Snowball the cat was curled up on Rose's pillow.

She was glad that Rose had pets. They looked over her. Just like she believed that Carol and Rick were looking over her.

"Help me, Carol, please," Lisa said, letting the tears fall from her eyes. She missed her sister so much; she couldn't imagine how Rose felt losing both her parents. "Help me to raise Rose right and get along with Sully."

Lisa wiped the tears from her eyes. There wasn't anything specific that triggered the tears. Maybe she was just tired.

They'd have a good time at Disney World. But it should

have been Carol and Rick taking their daughter there for the first time.

Lisa wasn't exactly the theme park type. She was more like NASA's Kennedy Space Center type, but that would bore Rose and Sully to death.

She resolved to try to have fun and act like a kid again, or at least a not-so-stuffy thirtysomething-year-old.

Sully wouldn't have a problem being a kid. That was his middle name.

Morning couldn't come fast enough. She wanted to get out of Fort Lauderdale. The sooner they left, the sooner they could get to Orlando and then back to Salmon Falls.

She figured that it would take about five hours to get to the park from Fort Lauderdale. In the morning, she'd call and get a reservation at the campground.

Sully would probably want to wing it, but she wasn't that type.

She drifted off to sleep wondering why Sully was always on her mind.

"I'm ready to go, Sully. It's oh-seven-thirty hours, and Rose and I have already had our breakfast."

Sully was tickling Rose, and Rose was laughing and screaming.

"So shall we get on the road?" she said, feeling like a stick-in-the-mud. Why couldn't she let Sully and Rose have a fun time together?

Probably because she felt like a third wheel.

"Sully, would you like some microwave oatmeal?"

"No offense, but I'd rather see what's on the communal buffet."

"I'll go for you," she said. "You can't walk yet."

She hurried to the food tent, amazed to find that a lot of motor homes had left already. She scooped some scrambled eggs onto a paper plate and added bacon and a bagel. That should keep Sully happy for a while.

She didn't have anything to contribute, so she left ten dollars in the coffee can marked "Donations."

Lisa took a deep breath and opened the door of the RV. Sully and Rose hadn't moved from their position on the dinette. They were watching a cartoon on TV, or rather Sully was. Rose was talking to her doll.

She handed Sully the plate of food along with a fork she pulled from the drawer.

"It looks like we're not going to leave on time," she said.

"Would it matter if we left at oh-eight-hundred and ten minutes?"

"I guess not," she snapped, then remembered her vow not to be so rigid. "Whenever you're ready." She poured herself a cup of coffee and sat down on the passenger's seat.

She watched Sully point out certain scenes of the cartoon and laugh with Rose. He fed scrambled eggs to Molly and scratched her behind the ears. She watched Rose ruffle Sully's hair and eat some of his bagel.

Lisa sat alone in the front of the RV, waiting to hit the road. She organized her purse and pulled out her calendar.

She forgot that she had to cancel her charter to Vegas from Albany, New York, the same weekend as the Anaheim event! She was looking forward to flying again, but Sully had to ride to get to the top.

"Something wrong?" Sully asked, holding up a strip of bacon.

"I forgot something. Something important."

"Can we pick it up along the way?" he asked.

"No. It's not that kind of thing.

"I'll be right back," she told Sully, slipping out of the motor home.

Her first call was for a campground reservation.

Her second call was to her pal Luann at JFW Aviation to tell her that she couldn't fly the charter.

She didn't have any other choice.

Sully could sense that there was something wrong with Lisa. She wasn't usually a ball of sunshine, but this was bad even for her.

Was it because he was playing with Rose and wasn't adhering to her departure schedule? Gee, he hadn't been able to play with Rose most of yesterday, and he missed her.

Would it kill her to wait a bit?

Probably.

"I have to get up, kiddo," he said to Rose. "Could you move a bit to let Uncle Sully up?"

"Okeydokey."

Sully pulled himself out of the dinette and took the melted ice off his ankle. He hopped to the bathroom.

One look told him that he needed a shave, but he didn't have the energy. Nor did he have the energy to take a shower.

He took a look at his ankle. It was twice the size of the other one, and Lisa was right—it was purple and swollen. He had to do what the doc told him to do: stay off it and keep it iced.

He had to ride this weekend in Connecticut even if it was still swollen and purple. He was number six in the standings thanks to his win last night, and he had to move up even higher.

He heard Lisa return to the RV and put the dinette back. He could hear her talking to Rose, who was helping her fold the sheets and blankets.

"Great job, sweetie!" Lisa said. "Are you excited to see all your cartoon friends today?"

"Yesss!"

"Okay. We'll get going just as soon as Uncle Sully is ready."

He'd better get his ass in gear.

He hurried as much as he could, deciding to keep his shorts on, but he needed a shirt.

Hopping to the bedroom, he waved to them. "I'm just getting a shirt, and we can leave."

"Okay," Lisa said.

He grabbed a PBR T-shirt and slipped it on. To be helpful, he made up the bed in the room. It looked like no one had slept in it, so it wasn't hard to do.

He put on some flip-flops and then noticed a pair of crutches on the bottom of his closet. He couldn't remember the last time he'd needed crutches. Oh yeah, he'd broken his leg at the Billings event a few years back.

He hopped out of the bedroom. "Let's rock, ladies. Time to visit all of Rose's pals."

Rose let out a shriek of excitement.

"Did you disconnect the water and the sewage?" he asked Lisa.

"Uh, no. I didn't think—"

"And the awning has to be taken in. The highway patrol might frown on us driving with it open."

"Of course."

They were common mistakes for rookie RVers, but Lisa seemed rattled. "If you did a walk around like you do with a plane, you might have noticed things still connected," he joked, trying to relieve her nervousness.

"If you would have moved your butt and helped me, maybe I would have known… Oh, forget it," she said through gritted teeth. "Would you mind sticking your head out the door and giving me some help?"

"No problem."

He led her through the unhooking procedures, and she

was a quick study. He hit a button for the awning from the inside, and it retracted.

"Brilliant," she said sarcastically.

"We're all set to go now."

She checked her watch. "Oh-nine-thirty hours. An hour and a half after I wanted to leave."

He knew that she'd bring up again that they were running late.

"Well, what's taking you so long? We're burning daylight."

He tossed her the keys, handed her the GPS and filled his ice pack.

Making sure that Rose was buckled in and had a tableful of books and toys, he took the passenger's seat. "It's only about four hours to Orlando from here."

"Five," she snapped.

"Okay, five. Relax, Lisa. We'll get there without going crazy."

She nodded.

"Turn the ignition on, Lisa."

"C'mon, Sully."

"Well, you need to turn the key."

"I know that!"

"What's stopping you?" he asked, puzzled.

"I just need to get my bearings."

"It's an automatic transmission, just like a car. All you have to do is just drive forward. No one is in front of you."

"I know. I know."

She was scared, he realized. But why? The woman flew jets, for heaven's sake, and she was scared of a thirty-foot motor home.

"Talk to me, Lisa," he said gently.

"It's like a bus. A huge bus. I have to navigate this thing on roads. But flying, in the sky, it's just…different."

"You can do it. I'll be your air traffic controller or, in this case, your earth traffic controller."

She laughed, and the tension seemed to evaporate. Finally, she turned the key and drove out of the parking lot and onto the highway as if she'd done it a thousand times.

"Piece of cake," Sully said.

"Yeah, I know."

"No. I wish I had a piece of cake. Chocolate."

She laughed again. "Sully, just set the GPS for the campgrounds. I jotted down the address in the back of my appointment book. It's in my purse."

After Sully found the address and set the navigation system, he found himself still holding Lisa's appointment book. He noticed an entry for a week from Saturday: Charter from Albany to Las Vegas.

"Lisa? Are you scheduled to fly a charter?"

No answer.

He sat back down in the passenger's seat. "Lisa? Talk to me."

"Yes, I was scheduled to fly a charter, but I cancelled it because you have to ride, and I have to take care of Rose, so I called my friend, Luann and asked her to keep me in mind for another charter flying out of Albany, New York. So I don't know when I'm going to fly again. Happy?"

"Hell, no. I'm not happy. I thought we were going to work things out," Sully said, thinking about her tirade. "Why didn't you tell me about the charter? You said you forgot?"

"I guess I did."

The GPS told Lisa to turn left, and she made a perfect turn.

"Forget it," she said.

"We could have worked it out."

She was silent for a while. "I really and truly forgot, Sully. I guess I was actually having a good time."

"Oh, no! A good time? How awful!"

She smiled. "After I got over my meltdown, comparing my communal life to a gathering of your friends, I began to have a good time. Everyone is so nice and friendly. And before you ask, that includes Chase Gatlin."

"He's okay," Sully admitted. "But I'm going to knock him out of first place."

"I hope you do."

"We need to discuss the Connecticut event this weekend," he said.

"If you think you can ride, I'll take care of Rose. From Salmon Falls you can make it to Connecticut in about five hours," she said. "Can you get a ride there so you don't have to drive?"

"I probably could."

"I could drive you but I really should keep Rose in Salmon Falls. She needs to be home again. And aren't we expecting a surprise visit at some point from the lawyer?"

"I forgot about the lawyer."

"I think we should have told him that we left with Rose."

"You're probably right. That's a big strike against us, huh?"

"Sully, I think we have more strikes against us than just not calling the lawyer."

"No, we don't. I think we're doing great. Rose had a good time at the PBR, and she'll have an even better time at the theme park."

"That's just stuff, Sully. We have to raise her. We have to get serious."

He shook his head. "How can I convince you that a little girl needs to have fun? She's had enough seriousness. She needs to laugh and run and splash and giggle."

"I know all that, Sully, but there's day care and preschool.

She can play with kids her own age and learn while she's at it."

"There's time for that stuff when she starts kindergarten."

"If she goes to preschool, she'll have a head start in kindergarten."

"Who cares? I didn't go to preschool and I'm doing okay," he said.

Lisa passed a slow-moving farm truck. "I won't even answer that."

"Did you go to preschool?" he asked.

"I was raised in a commune, remember? School was sitting on a blanket talking about everything *but* academics. When I went to regular school in seventh grade, because my parents were 'between communes,' I was hideously behind. I don't want Rose to be behind."

"She's three years old. She needs to enjoy being three!" he said.

"You aren't listening to me."

His ankle was throbbing, and his brain was throbbing. "You aren't listening to me either. She should enjoy her young years. There's plenty of time for school later. Let her have fun. She's been dealt a bad hand."

He lifted his leg and stretched it out on his gear bag to elevate his ankle and wondered if they'd ever reach a compromise on this one.

Chapter Eleven

They rolled into the campgrounds a few hours later, no thanks to Sully. He had fallen asleep while sitting across from Rose at the dinette.

"Where's my dolly? Where is Princess Mary Ann?" That was the first thing that penetrated his brain. "Aunt Lisa, Uncle Sully, where's my princess dolly? I lost her." Once they were stopped, Rose unhooked the seat belt of her car seat in one fast movement and scrambled out of the dinette.

Sully pulled a doll out from behind his back. "I must be like the princess who slept on a pea. I could feel something in my back when I was sleeping."

Rose giggled and Lisa swallowed a smile.

"I hope Princess Mary Ann is okay." He smoothed down the doll's scraggly hair and wrinkled pink gown and handed the beloved Mary Ann to Rose. "Oh, wait…she's missing a shoe."

Sully felt around the dinette and turned up a small

white plastic heel. He studied it for a while before handing it to Rose.

"Thank you, Uncle Sully," Rose said, slipping the heel on Princess Mary Ann's foot.

"I'm going to check us in at the office," Lisa said.

"Lisa, wait." Sully reached for his wallet and handed Lisa a credit card. "This is for the campground cost."

Lisa waved him away, although she was impressed by his thoughtfulness. "It's on me."

"No way. I'm the big PBR winner." He pumped the air with a fist. "Let me buy."

She thought for a while. "We really should have a mutual account, Sully."

"We'll do that later, but for now, I'd like this to be my treat."

She smiled slightly and took his credit card. "We thank you."

"I have to put my special dress on," Rose declared, running into the bedroom. "And my special sandals."

As Lisa walked down the stairs of the RV to check in, she remembered her vow to lighten up. She needed this time away. She wanted to enjoy it with Rose and Sully.

"Rose, you have to buckle in," Lisa stated when she returned. "I'm going to drive us to our campsite now."

"I'm not dressed yet," Rose replied.

"You can finish later. Let Uncle Sully help you buckle in."

Lisa waited until Sully gave her the sign that Rose was ready. Soon she was driving into their site, which was surrounded by a copse of trees. She pushed the button to lower the awning. "Sully, I'll hook up the hoses."

"Remember how?" He stood with his crutches.

"Of course! I'm a seasoned RV-er now!"

It didn't take her long to get the RV ready. It was as if she'd done it a million times before. She liked their site with grass, palm trees and other conifers. There was a picnic table and a grill.

Lisa wanted a cookout, complete with steaks and potato and macaroni salads. She hadn't had a cookout since she'd left the commune—if you could call that a cookout. The steak probably had been some sort of mushroom and soybean concoction.

When they drove in, she had seen a camp store and hoped that they sold real meat with all the fixings. If Sully could get the grill going, she could cook the steaks.

She took a deep breath of the pine-scented air. The campground had a cute swimming area that Rose would love and so would Lisa. Sully would probably love it the most.

Walking up the stairs into the RV, she saw that Sully was buckling Rose's sandals. She looked so cute with her pretty pink dress, which was similar to Princess Mary Ann's.

"Rose, will you let Uncle Sully brush your hair? Maybe put it in ponytails?"

Sully looked as if snakes were coming out of Lisa's head. "You want me to brush her hair?"

"And put it in ponytails," Lisa instructed. "You can handle it. I'm going to change into shorts."

Sully didn't move but stared at Rose wide-eyed.

"Rose, sweetie, help Uncle Sully. I think he's more scared of doing your hair than riding a big bull."

Rose giggled, then pulled out a brush from her little plastic purse and handed it to him.

"I have rubber bands, too, Uncle Sully."

"Okay."

Lisa left the door of the bedroom open a crack. She wasn't going to miss this for the world.

Rose sat on Sully's lap. "Okay, go."

He gently began to brush her hair, but every now and then she let out an "ouch," which flustered Sully.

"Are you okay?" he asked her.

"It just hurts."

"I'm sorry, sweetie, but your hair is a mess."

Finally, all the knots were out, but the more he brushed, the more it became loaded with static.

Lisa should probably tell him to wet it, but she was too busy laughing.

The look on Sully's face was priceless. "Um…Rose, I have a mess going on here. Your hair is sticking up all over the place."

She touched her hair and made a face. "Oh, Uncle Sully!"

"Don't you worry a bit. I'm going to corral your hair into ponytails. It'll be fine. Now hand me a rubber band."

Lisa couldn't help but laugh as she changed into a pair of khaki shorts and a short-sleeved blouse.

Sully had put one ponytail on top of Rose's head and one down toward her ear.

"What do you think, Rose?"

She looked into a little hand mirror. "They're crooked."

"Naw, the motor home is parked on a slant. Your ponytails will be perfect when we step outside."

Rose thought about this for a while, then shook her head, giggling. One of the ponytails came loose.

"I think that Aunt Lisa has to come to the rescue," he said. "Maybe she can show me where I went wrong. Then I'll do better next time."

Lisa stepped out of the bedroom. "Rose's hair is very fine. Wet her hair next time. It'll be easier to handle. Now watch."

Lisa took Rose over to the sink and wet her hair a bit. "Now, you divide her hair into two sections. And you pull up the ponytail at the same location on both sides."

Lisa remembered standing in front of the bathhouse mirrors at one of the communes and helping her sister Carol put her hair into ponytails. Then Carol would do the same for

Lisa. After, they would slip into their gauzy white dresses and go outside to start their day, doing pretty much nothing.

Who would have thought that Lisa would be doing the hair of Carol's daughter?

Tears stung her eyes, and Lisa blinked them back. She didn't want anyone to see her cry. They were at the happiest place on Earth, and they all needed some happiness.

She pulled Rose into a hug. "I love you. You know that, Rose?"

"Yes."

"And Uncle Sully loves you," Lisa said, still hugging Rose to her.

"Uh-huh," said Rose, hugging Lisa back.

"Now let's go to the park."

She handed Sully his crutches, and they all left the motor home.

"That was nice of you to include me, Lisa," Sully said as Rose skipped ahead.

"Of course I'd include you. We're a…a…family."

He put his arm around her shoulders, balancing on his crutches, and she felt a jolt of pleasure rush through her.

He quickly returned his hand to his crutch. "Oh, sorry. I didn't mean to do that. It just happened."

"No, no. It's okay." She wanted to tell him that she liked his arm around her, but it was a moot point now. She'd scared him off.

They'd both discussed their relationship, and both made it clear that they were just friends working toward a common goal—the raising of Rose. That's all.

They were too different to be anything more than just friends, Lisa thought, and the last thing they both needed was more complications.

Friends. That's all they'd ever be.

Then why was she feeling an overwhelming pull toward Sully?

* * *

Sully grinned. Watching Rose run around the park was something he'd always remember.

Right now the girl was talking to one of the characters while Sully stood nearby. He could see that Lisa was softly crying off to the side. She'd stepped away from the crowd but was still close enough to hear, and she kept brushing the tears from her cheeks.

"My mommy and daddy are in heaven," he heard Rose tell the costumed character. "Aunt Lisa and Uncle Sully are taking care of me. I watch your movies—all of them."

They talked about her movies and her prince, who apparently was getting ready for the parade later. Rose just glowed.

Too soon, it was time for the next little girl in line, and Rose had to move on. Sully took her hand and led her away with the promise of going swimming later.

Lisa joined them. Her eyes were red-rimmed and the tip of her nose was red, but she grinned widely at Rose.

"Wasn't that fun?" she asked.

"She's so pretty!" Rose said.

"So are you, sweetie." Lisa bent over and enveloped Rose in a big hug.

The child hugged her back. "Can I ride the merry-go-round?"

"Of course you can," Lisa said, meeting Sully's gaze.

Rose began skipping. Luckily, she was skipping in the right direction. Sully was disappointed that he had to be confined to crutches. His foot was throbbing, and he really should have rented an electric wheelchair, but there had been none left.

"C'mon, Lisa. Skip with Rose," he said over his shoulder.

She seemed to be debating with herself. Then she moved, slowly.

"Rose, wait up! You have to teach Aunt Lisa how to skip." Lisa hurried to catch up with her.

The little girl took Lisa's hand and showed her how to move up and down with a little hop.

"It's like riding a bike," Lisa said. "I remember now."

"Let's go!" Sully said.

Lisa looked around to see who was watching.

"Don't worry about who's watching. Just do it," Sully said.

The two of them locked hands and they skipped, right in the middle of the walkway.

When they stopped, he noticed the flushed, but happy, expression on Lisa's face. At this moment she was a far cry from the stuffy, uptight woman that he knew.

They walked the rest of the way next to him, stopping to look at different attractions. Lisa marveled at the cups and saucers.

"I have to go on that," she said. "Rose, what do you think?"

"I want to go on that, too." She took Sully's hand. "C'mon, Uncle Sully."

"I'm in."

They waited in line, and he tried not to look like he was in pain. He didn't wait to ruin their good time. They both needed fun and laughs.

When it was their turn, Rose scrambled to get a pink teacup.

He joined them, handing Lisa his crutches and sitting down. He put his leg up on the seat across from him with an involuntary grunt.

"You must be hurting, Sully," Lisa said. "Too bad they didn't have any electric wheelchairs left to rent."

"I'm okay. Don't worry about me. Just have fun," he

said. He helped them turn the wheel on the cup until they screamed for him to stop. Laughing, they turned it some more.

He wished he had a camera to capture the memories. He'd never thought of bringing one. However, he had a feeling that he'd never forget this trip.

The ride stopped and they climbed out of the cup. Next stop was the merry-go-round.

By the time Lisa had gotten Rose settled on a pink and blue horse, Sully thought his foot was going to explode. After she rode twice, he proposed they find a restaurant and eat. They found a reservation phone and were able to get a table for three at a character buffet at one of the restaurants.

Rose was so excited that she barely ate.

Lisa, either.

He, however, ate enough for all of them.

While they dined, the characters appeared. They sang a song together, much to the delight of the children and to a round of applause.

Lisa clapped the hardest.

"Why don't we have a camera?" Lisa asked him. "Or a cell phone with one?"

"Yeah, I know."

"Oh well. I think Rose is getting tired," Lisa said.

"Maybe we can go back to the motor home and she'll take a nap," Sully said.

"We can try. She's pretty exhausted."

They took a bus back to the campgrounds. They put Rose to bed in the bedroom, and Sully settled in on the passenger side with his foot propped on his gear bag.

"Sully, I'm going to go for a swim."

"Okay," he mumbled.

He registered Lisa leaving in a turquoise one-piece bathing suit that she'd bought at a gift shop at the park. It clung in all the right places. He'd never realized how long her legs were or how her hair fell down her back in layers of gold.

She wrapped a striped towel around herself and tied it in a knot over her breasts.

She still looked hot.

"I won't be long," she said.

"Take your time. Enjoy yourself."

"You know, Sully, I haven't had this good a time in a long while."

"Wish we could stay here longer."

"Yeah, I know."

"Some other time, huh?" he asked.

She nodded and left for her swim.

The motor home felt lonely with her gone.

Lisa did laps, swung from ropes into the water, floated on a tube and slid down a long, twisting and turning slide that ended with a plunge into the water.

She hadn't felt this good in a long time.

Grabbing a tube, she hopped up on it and looked at the deep-blue sky. Clouds as fluffy as cotton candy floated by and she thought of what each shape reminded her of.

She used to do the same thing at the commune. It was what she did to pass the time. Sometimes, she'd made up stories about the clouds.

Now, if she made up a story, it would be that she, Rose and Sully would become a family and live happily ever after, just like a perfect fairy tale.

She thought of her sister again.

"I wish you could have seen Rose's face," she said to Carol. "She's so happy here."

Lisa vowed to make Rose just as happy in the big Victorian in Salmon Falls.

* * *

Sully and Rose waved to Lisa from the shallow water, but she was floating on a tube, looking up at the sky and didn't see them.

She seemed relaxed and content.

"Can you take me out to Aunt Lisa, Uncle Sully?"

He probably could. He was buoyant in the water, and his foot actually felt good.

"Sure, sweetie."

He held Rose in front of him, and she made like she was swimming.

"You're doing a great job swimming, but don't forget to kick your feet."

As they got close to Lisa, he whispered in Rose's ear that she should grip Lisa's toe.

Rose did, and Lisa let out a scream that probably scared the birds from the trees in every county in Florida.

Lisa laughed when she saw who it was. Standing, she held out her hands, and with an excited whoop, Rose jumped into them. Sully grabbed her tube, and flopped onto it.

He enjoyed watching Lisa play with Rose. She twirled her around in the water and tried to teach her to float on her back and blow bubbles in the water.

He thought again how much Lisa was enjoying this trip.

Maybe he should put a pool in the backyard. He'd talk to Lisa about it. Or maybe there were swimming lessons at a nearby pool for Rose in the interim.

"How's your ankle?" Lisa asked him.

"It feels good to get off my feet for a while."

He didn't know why she kept asking him about his injury. He'd had much worse.

"Sully, I've been meaning to talk to you about something."

"What's that?"

"Um…" She shifted her eyes toward Rose. "What about if we…uh…stay another…"

He got her message: She wanted to stay another day. But that meant more consecutive hours on the road, hours that she would have to drive. Nah, the hell with it. He could drive.

"Let's do it. Rose is having a ball."

"The PBR was fun, too. So was camping in the parking lot—that was a first for me—and meeting your friends."

"Especially Tiffany?" he joked.

"Especially Chase Gatlin!"

He felt a quick stab of jealousy before he realized that she was joking back.

He held his hand up for a high five, and she slapped it.

"Good one," he said.

"I know!"

She held Rose under her arms and twirled her around in the water. Rose giggled. "More!"

"Time out for me," Lisa said. "I'm going to get out and dry off. Then I'm going to hike up to the camp store and get some marshmallows, a couple of steaks and some salads. We can have a cookout tomorrow. Okay?"

"We can have the marshmallows tonight," he said. "Rose would like toasted marshmallows."

Who was he kidding? Rose would be sleeping before he lit the grill.

But he was always up for some marshmallows toasted over a campfire. Lisa's company would be an added bonus.

This might be his lucky night…er…not that kind of lucky, but maybe he and Lisa could continue to have good conversations and even enjoy each other's company a little bit more.

Chapter Twelve

The store was just about to close by the time Lisa got there, but she was able to get what she'd wanted along with a couple of slices of apple pie. Unfortunately, they were out of marshmallows until tomorrow.

"No marshmallows?" Sully asked, sticking his bottom lip out like a kid.

"Oh stop it!" She laughed. "I do have pie, however."

"It'll do."

While she was putting everything away in the RV for their cookout tomorrow, Rose began to doze off, and Lisa helped her change into her nightgown and get settled on the big bed.

When she went back outside, Sully had a campfire going and had pulled out two lawn chairs. She handed him a piece of pie and a travel mug of black coffee.

"Thanks," he said.

"This is heaven." She looked up at the sky full of bright

stars. "A full moon, a campfire and apple pie, and we showed our niece a great time."

"You had a great time, too."

"I really did. I haven't had such a great time in a long time." She laughed. "Did that make sense?"

"It did. I'm glad you're enjoying yourself. Also, you've done a world of good for Rose."

"Thanks. That means a lot to me to hear you say that. But you've done a world of good for Rose, too. She just adores you."

He didn't respond, but Lisa could tell he was pleased.

"We have three days to get back to Salmon Falls. Then, I have to take off for Connecticut." Sully took a deep breath, then let it out slowly. "You know, I'm going to hate to leave you alone with Rose."

"I'll manage."

Sully stared into the fire.

"Are you feeling guilty, Sully?"

"Sure am, but I really appreciate being able to ride."

"You know, I think we had this conversation before, so stop feeling guilty." She was surprised that Sully even knew the word. In the past, he had worried about nothing but a good time. "And remember that you're not riding in the summer, so I'll do some charter flying then. Right?"

"Right." He snapped his fingers. "I've been meaning to ask you something. When are you going to finally admit that you watch me on TV?"

By the glow of the campfire, she could see the smile on his face. So, he wanted to tease her, huh?

"I'll admit that I enjoy watching bull riding. It's one of the few sports that I like, other than figure skating and snowboarding."

"That's quite the broad range of sports." He chuckled.

"But let's get back to bull riding. Did you say something before about how you tape the PBR when you're out of town? Is that so you can watch me ride over and over again?"

"Don't flatter yourself." She made a noise in the back of her throat. "Actually, I said that I tape it so I can watch Chase Gatlin ride over and over again."

He almost choked on his pie.

"Good one, Lisa. Good one."

"I thought so," she said smugly.

"But." Sully held his hand up. "You didn't know Chase until the other day."

"Maybe not in person, but I know him from watching bull riding on TV. He's right up there in the rankings. Oh wait, isn't he higher than you?" She smiled widely, then blew him a kiss.

"Not after last weekend. He dropped like a rock." Sully grinned just like she had, made like he was grabbing her kiss from the air and then put it on his cheek. "Nice kiss, but you can do better," he said.

Her cheeks heated, but she blamed it on the fire.

"So, Lisa, can't you just admit that you watch me on TV?"

"Sure, I'll admit it if it makes you feel better."

He leaned over and rested his arms on his legs. "I guess I'll never get a straight answer out of you."

She listened to the crackling of the fire for a while. Sully was silent, and she could feel the tension in the air.

"What do you want me to say? That I like watching you ride? That I like watching clips of you patiently signing autographs for kids and posing for pictures with them? That I've seen features of you with kids in Western Wishes whose big wish was to spend the day with you behind the chutes?"

He met her gaze. "If you think I do those things for the publicity, you're completely wrong."

"To be honest, I did at first, but then I changed my mind."

He tossed a log on the fire, and the sparks flew into the air. "You must really think I'm a jerk."

"I thought you were worse than a jerk, Sully. And you did nothing to prove me wrong back then. But I have really and truly changed my mind."

"So, I'm upgraded to what? Idiot?"

"No. Not at all. I'm just trying to get to know you better now. The way you are *right now*. And you can't tell me that you've always liked me, either."

He laughed. "I called you Ice Queen."

"I hope I've thawed out some."

"You have."

"Is there anything more we should discuss?" Lisa asked. "It seems like a perfect environment for us to talk."

"Are you still going to enroll Rose in an accelerated college program when we get back?" He took a sip of coffee. "How about Harvard?"

"I know you're concerned about Rose not having any fun as a child and going right to school, but it's nursery school. She'll be jumping rope and coloring and learning the alphabet and numbers. It'll be fun for her."

"Help me to understand why she needs a school for that. We can play with her and teach her."

"Sully, we aren't professionals. In school, she'll meet kids her own age. It's important for her to have friends, you know for play dates and all."

"There aren't any kids in the neighborhood?"

"Probably, but they're all in nursery school."

He grunted. "Hmm…"

"It's important that she goes to an organized school."

"You mean that it's important to *you*."

"Yeah, okay. It's important to me," she snapped.

"Because of the communes you lived in?"

She nodded. "Let's just visit the school. Maybe you'll change your mind."

"Or maybe you will."

She shrugged. "I doubt it."

"Okay. In the spirit of cooperation, I'll agree to visit the nursery school with you," he said. "And I'll keep an open mind."

On a whim, she kissed his cheek. This was a big compromise for him.

"We're doing pretty good, aren't we, Sully?"

"I think we're doing great." He took her hand and played with her fingers. It seemed like too intimate a gesture for the two of them, but she had to admit that she liked it. It felt as if they shared a connection together, like they were in this together, which they were. "I just hope Glen Randolph will think we're doing great, too."

"Oh, shoot," Lisa said. "I forgot about him again. I hope he hasn't been looking for us since we didn't tell him we were going on this trip."

"Big mistake on our part."

"I keep forgetting to call him," she said. "But you know, you could have."

"Isn't it your job to do that kind of thing?" He held her hand tightly because he probably knew that she was going to slug him with it. "Just kidding. I like to get a rise out of you."

"I know."

The fire was dying, and Sully didn't make a move to put their final log on.

"I think I'm going to call it a night," Lisa said. "I have about two square feet of bed that's calling my name."

He laughed. "That's all the room you get? It's a queen bed."

"Rose can really travel at night. So does Molly and Snowball. And last night, Princess Mary Ann got stuck in my hair."

"Ouch." Sully didn't let go of her hand but helped her out of her chair while balancing on one crutch.

Lisa couldn't believe the strength in Sully's riding arm when he pulled her up. She ended up standing a little too close to him.

"Lisa?" he said.

She could smell the coffee on his breath and the smoke of the campfire on his shirt. She found herself holding her breath, waiting. Her heart pounded against her chest, and she didn't want to meet his eyes, afraid of what might come next.

She wasn't ready, yet she was.

"Sully?" she whispered.

It would take barely a step to close the distance between them, but she couldn't move. It would be the biggest step of her life.

Sully and her?

Impossible.

Her opinion of him was gradually changing. He made her laugh, he challenged her and he was one sexy cowboy.

Oh, for heaven's sake, he was going to kiss her.

No! He shouldn't. He wouldn't dare.

A kiss would change everything.

He put his arm around her and pulled her toward him, giving her time to move away.

She didn't know if it was the magic of the night or just the magic of Sully, but she tilted her head and met his lips with hers.

And she was floating, her heart was singing, and she felt like she could touch the stars. This was Brett Sullivan kissing her and, yes, she'd probably had a secret crush on him for too many years.

Darn him!

What the hell was he doing kissing Lisa Phillips?

About the second kiss, it hit him that her lips were soft and malleable. During the third kiss, he noticed that she made the sweetest sounds. After the fourth kiss, he realized that he was falling for Lisa Phillips—the Ice Queen—and that had been the most flattering of all his nicknames for her.

He wished he didn't need the one crutch so he could put both arms around her. She felt perfect crushed to him, and he'd thought about kissing her throughout the years, but he'd quickly come to his senses. The Ice Queen wasn't his type at all.

"Sully, what the hell are we doing?" Lisa stepped back, and he wanted to close the space between them again. He wasn't finished yet.

"What the hell are we doing?" He chuckled. "Kissing?"

"You know what I mean. Why are we kissing?"

"Because we wanted to?"

He noticed that she still had her hand on his shoulder, and he still had his hand on her waist.

She shrugged. "Maybe."

"We could blame it on this special place. Or maybe on a beautiful night and a beautiful woman? Maybe we've been secretly attracted to each other throughout the years. Or maybe our attraction is a recent thing."

She was silent for a while, staring off into the darkness. "I don't think it's a good idea for us to get involved. What if it didn't work out, or if we had a bad breakup? We'd still have to raise Rose together and live together, and it would be very uncomfortable. Rose would pick up on our friction, and it wouldn't be healthy for her."

"It was only a couple of kisses, Lisa! You already have us broken up and Rose in psychiatric treatment. You're over-thinking things."

"And you don't think things through enough."

"I certainly will from now on!" He'd never had such a strange conversation after kissing a woman. He'd hate to think what she'd say after they made love.

He froze. Made love? That was as unlikely as snow in Orlando.

"I'm sorry, Sully," she said. "I don't know what came over me. I'm probably not like the other women...um... that you've kissed."

He didn't say anything. He didn't know how to answer that other than by saying, "Damn straight!"

"But you have to admit that we are in a peculiar situa-tion. We have to tread carefully. We have to think long term and we have to think of Rose."

"We're not allowed to have our own needs? Our own lives?"

"Well, yes. Sure."

He raised an eyebrow. "When can we start?"

"When Rose is eighteen, I guess. It'll be less compli-cated."

"I'll set my watch."

Lisa crawled in bed with Rose. Snowball and Molly were at the foot of the bed, and Princess Mary Ann was in place on Rose's pillow.

All was the same, but everything had changed.

What a night!

She and Sully had had pie along with a nice conversa-tion about each other, Rose and nursery school. At least he'd agreed to take a look at the school. That was a big deal for him.

Then they'd kissed.

And kissed some more.

Lisa felt a fluttering in her stomach just thinking about Sully. That was just what she didn't want to happen. She didn't want him on her mind 24/7.

She did overthink things. Sully was right about that. But she couldn't help herself. She was an intelligent woman, not one of his buckle bunnies.

Tossing and turning all night, she counted Rose's breaths instead of sheep. She petted Snowball for so long that she thought that the cat would soon be bald.

Still she couldn't sleep.

She must have drifted off around dawn, just about the time they were going to hit the road.

She heard Sully moving around, then a big crash and a thud that woke up Rose and the menagerie.

"Stay here, sweetie. Go back to sleep," Lisa told her, fixing her covers.

Lisa sprang out of bed, went into the kitchen and found Sully face down on the kitchen floor.

"Sully? Are you okay?"

"I'm okay. I just tripped over my crutch. It must have fallen during the night."

He flipped over onto his back and winced.

"What else did you hurt?"

"Both of my elbows. I hit the floor elbows first." He swore under his breath. "You'd think I'd know how to fall by now. I've had enough practice, but this took me by surprise."

"Let me help you," Lisa said. She picked up the crutch that he'd tripped over and handed it to him to use as leverage.

With several grunts from both of them, he was able to get up. She handed him his other crutch, and he headed for the bathroom. Lisa decided to make a pot of coffee because she'd never be able to go back to sleep now.

He returned and collapsed on the dinette bed.

"Do you need a doctor? A hospital?" Lisa asked.

"Nah."

"Tough guy."

He chuckled. "Coffee smells good. Do you mind pouring me a cup?"

"Coming up."

She handed him a cup of coffee, black. "I was thinking… maybe we should have a party for Rose's birthday."

"Absolutely," Sully said.

"Yes." She liked that he wanted to have a party for Rose's birthday, but then of course he would.

Sully sat down on the passenger's seat. "We'll have a barbecue for her birthday. I make a mean rack of ribs, and then there's always hot dogs and hamburgers for the kids."

"We have a lot of time to plan her party, but right now, we have to think about breakfast. I'll call and see if we can land a character breakfast. After that, we can find out where and when the characters are appearing. What else?"

"The rides," Sully said. "And I'm going to buy a camera somewhere, first thing."

"I saw them in the store right here in the campgrounds."

"Excellent," Sully said. "And then we'll do your steak barbecue for dinner."

"I can taste it already!"

"Smile," Sully said, taking yet another picture. This time it was of she and Rose eating an ice cream.

He clicked away when they were on the rides; when Rose was with the characters; when she was in front of bright flowers, topiaries and fountains and sitting on the grass.

Finally, Lisa took the camera away from him and did

some clicking of her own, so he could be in some of the pictures.

"Let me try it," Rose asked. "Please? Can I?"

Sully nodded. "Take a picture of Aunt Lisa and me."

He patiently showed her what to push and where to look.

"Okay!" she said impatiently. "Stand together."

They did.

"Can you see us?" Sully asked.

"Yes," she said.

"Okay. Then click the button."

She did, and when Sully and Lisa went to look, the picture was perfect.

"Let me do another one!" Rose said.

"No. That's enough." Sully took the camera from her and she began to pout. She crossed her arms, and stomped her foot. Then she sat down on the ground.

Sully looked at Lisa with raised brows, palms in the air.

Rose was such a sweet, even-tempered little girl, and she rarely showed any sign of being contrary. She was definitely tired. It was time to go back to the campground for a nap.

Lisa nodded toward Rose, then motioned for Sully to handle her. It was time for him to be the disciplinarian for once.

"Rose, get up off the ground. You are getting dirty," he said.

"I don't want to."

"Sweetie, I'm telling you to get up, or there will be nothing but bread and water for you tonight or maybe gruel."

"Gruel?" Lisa asked, trying not to laugh. "You've watched Oliver Twist too many times."

"Honey, would you like some cotton candy? I'll get you some cotton candy if you get up," Sully said.

"No!"

He looked at Lisa. "Now what?"

"Try again."

This time he held out his hand to her. "Let's go back to the RV, Rose. Uncle Sully is awful tired, and I have to rest my ankle. Are you tired, too?"

"Maybe," she said, taking his hand.

Lisa took Rose's other hand. "I'm pretty tired, too."

"Let's take a boat back," Sully said. "Okay, Rose?"

"Yes!"

On the boat ride, Rose fell asleep across their laps, and, as he stared down at the doll-like face of his little niece, Sully felt like a real father.

The next morning, Lisa walked out of the bedroom into the main cabin of the RV. She smelled coffee and saw Sully was awake. He was wearing red gym shorts and pouring himself a cup of coffee.

"Morning," she said.

"Morning."

"I think we have to get back to Salmon Falls. Shall I get the motor home ready?" Lisa whispered, closing the bedroom door behind her.

Sully nodded. "We're both up, so we might as well rock and roll."

"What about Rose? Should we wake her up so we can buckle her into the dinette?"

"Brilliant idea."

Lisa took a couple of sips of coffee, then went back into the bedroom to slip on a pair of slacks and a blouse to go outside. She disconnected the hoses and the electric hook-ups.

When she returned to the motor home, Rose and her pets had relocated to the dinette. She was still sleeping, but Lisa noticed that she was buckled in.

Sully had slipped on a T-shirt.

Too bad. He was buff, and Lisa enjoyed the view.

"Let's go home," she said, slipping behind the wheel.

Sully moved to the passenger's seat. He put both mugs of coffee into the slots in the console, reached for the GPS and began typing.

"We are going to one huge, white Victorian on twenty pretty acres in tiny Salmon Falls, New York. Got it."

Lisa set out for the campground office. She didn't know if they needed to check out, but she decided to stop anyway.

"Lisa, stop!" Sully shouted.

Her heart started to pound, and she hit the brakes.

"What's the matter?"

"We didn't retract the awning. We almost took out a couple of windows on some trailers. Luckily, we just clipped a few trees."

She put the RV in Park, got up and pushed the button. "I hope I didn't break anything."

"I don't think we actually hit anything hard. It's my fault. I don't know why I didn't remember. I *always* hit the awning button first." He chuckled. "I guess you're my distraction."

It was a joke and she was reading too much into it, but she didn't want to be his distraction. Nor did she want any references to their momentary loss of sanity last night.

"I'll tape a note to the steering wheel," she said. "It won't happen again."

"Relax, Lisa. It's an easy mistake."

"I don't make mistakes."

"Lisa, this isn't a plane. It's just a motor home."

"But still…"

"You're too hard on yourself. Give yourself a break."

She was just about to tell him that he was too easygoing, but she admired that about him. There were a lot of things she admired about Sully.

Among other things, he sure could kiss.

Not that she wanted him to, but she wondered if he'd ever kiss her again.

Chapter Thirteen

Two days later at three in the morning they pulled into the big Victorian in Salmon Falls.

Rose was cranky because they drove around the clock from the last campground in North Carolina. Lisa was pretty cranky herself. She had a pounding headache, and her eyes felt like they'd been through a sandstorm. She was so tired of driving, she didn't want to get behind the wheel for months.

Sully was still in good spirits. Then again, when wasn't he?

He was whistling as he unloaded the motor home.

"I'm hungry, Aunt Lisa," Rose said, near tears.

"I could make us a snack."

"Sounds good, but don't fuss," Sully said.

"I don't even know how to fuss," she muttered under her breath, taking mental inventory of the contents of the motor home refrigerator. "How about ham and cheese sandwiches?"

He hurried by, carrying bags full of laundry even while maneuvering his crutches. "Sounds good to me."

"Can I have grapes, too?" Rose asked.

"I can handle grapes," Lisa said. "Coming up."

She took a plastic bin and unloaded what she could carry from the fridge, including what she needed for their later-than-midnight snack.

Carrying it all into the kitchen, she put what she needed onto the counter and put the rest away.

She'd had a fabulous time, but it was great to be back in a house that didn't move.

"It's great to be home, isn't it?" Sully asked, putting more clothes in the laundry room.

"You read my mind."

"This is the first time I ever called a wood and vinyl building home. I always thought of my motor home as my home."

"I barely gave my apartment in Atlanta a thought as we drove through Georgia."

Sully removed his hat and slapped it on his knee. "I am so sorry. We could have picked up some more of your things. We were right there."

"We couldn't spare the time for the detour, so I didn't bring it up," she said.

"We could have spared the time," Sully said.

"I was too tired of driving, Sully. I just wanted to get home."

Aside from a couple of pieces of furniture she'd bought to augment what had come with the furnished apartment, all she had in her apartment were her Cardinal Global uniforms and her clothes.

If she wasn't going to be flying for Cardinal anymore, naturally, she'd have to give up her apartment.

They all sat around the table munching on sandwiches

and grapes. Sully popped the top on an orange soda, and they all shared that.

Rose could barely keep her eyes open to eat the rest of her sandwich.

"Time for bed, sweetie," Lisa said, giving Rose a kiss on the forehead.

"I'll get her ready," Sully volunteered.

"Thanks. I'll clean this up and take another trip to the motor home."

"Leave it. I plugged the rig in. Everything will be fine until tomorrow. We all need some sleep, especially you, Lisa. Go to bed."

"Thanks. Don't mind if I do."

Sully whistled softly, then made a high-pitched sound. Snowball and Molly followed them to Rose's room.

It was an effort to put one foot in front of the other, but Lisa finally made it to her room. She stared at the big, comfortable bed that she'd have all to herself.

She opened the windows to let some air in and collapsed on the bed, clothes and all.

One day later, it was time for Sully to go to Connecticut.

Rose clung to him like a piece of lint, her arms around his neck and her legs around his waist.

"Don't go, Uncle Sully. Don't go."

"I have to ride some bulls, you know that, Rosie-girl. You can watch me on TV tonight." His ride was waiting in the driveway—a cowboy by the name of Justin O'Day. Lisa liked him immediately.

Rose was crying loudly now. "I don't want a bull to step on you."

"I'll be extra careful, Rose. Extra careful. And I'll wave to you on TV. How's that?"

Her tears miraculously dried up. "You'll wave to me?"

"I sure will. Maybe I can even say your name. Won't that be fun?" he asked.

Rose nodded. "I'll watch you, Uncle Sully. Me and Aunt Lisa will watch you. We'll make popcorn and have grape juice, and we'll watch you."

"Now that sounds like fun! Too bad I have to go."

"It really is," Lisa said, "but I hope you win."

"Thanks."

"Now give me a kiss goodbye," Sully said, and Lisa looked at him wide-eyed. "I meant Rose. Relax, Lisa."

She chuckled and waved her hand, like she knew he'd meant Rose all along.

After Rose kissed him, Lisa gave him a chaste peck on the cheek. "For good luck," she said.

"I'll have double the luck now." He grinned.

"Go, you flatterer!"

He tossed his gear bag and his crutches into the flatbed, then settled into the passenger side of the silver truck.

"Don't forget to keep icing your ankle. And have it checked over by sports medicine again. And call Rose. And win. And have a good time but not that good of a time!"

He laughed. "I understand."

Justin O'Day took everything in stride. "Are we ready to go now, Sully?"

"I have to say goodbye to my family."

"I thought that's what you've been doing for the past hour."

"Give me more time, O'Day. More time."

"We need to get on the road soon," the young cowboy replied.

"One more thing." Sully took Lisa by the arm and led her away from Rose and Justin. "I just want to make sure you'll be okay with Rose alone."

"We'll be fine," she said. "But you'd better find a way to wave to Rose, or you'll be one sorry uncle!"

"I know. I just have to be a good enough rider to snag an interview."

"Go," she told Sully. "Justin is getting impatient."

"I can't imagine going to a hotel during an event instead of staying in my motor home."

"Such luxury!"

"Not with four or five riders sharing a room."

Memories of college dorm rooms came flooding back. "Ha! Good luck with that."

"That's one of the reasons I bought a motor home." He looked at his rig in the driveway. "Call me if you need me."

She held out her hand to him, and he took it. "We'll be fine."

"Take care of yourself and Rose." He hung on to her hand for what seemed like minutes. He was going to say something, but judging by the slight shake of his head, he changed his mind.

Lisa wondered what he might've said.

"I wanted to ask Lisa to come, Justin. I wanted us to go in the motor home again. Damn, I loved that Fort Lauderdale trip."

"Why didn't you ask her?" Justin asked.

"We decided that Rose needed stability. She needed to stay put."

"Wouldn't Rose be more stable with both of you together?"

"Aw, hell, I don't know. She was so clingy and upset, I wonder if she thought I wasn't coming back, like her father."

"Could be. Lisa had to pry her off you," Justin said.

Sully sighed. "I'm not good at this father thing."

"It's hard to mix a family with a job that requires a lot

of travel, Sully. You have to just give in and fly so you can spend more time at home. After Connecticut, the next event is Anaheim. What are you going to do then? Spend five days to get there and five days back?"

His heart pounded a loud tattoo in his chest, and he couldn't breathe, couldn't swallow. Just how did those huge things stay in the sky?

He sighed. He had to fly for both Lisa and Rose's sake, but maybe there was another way. A train, maybe.

"I think you may be right, pard, but I just can't bring myself to fly."

The mail was stuffed to the max in the mailbox at the end of the driveway. Lisa wished she'd brought a bag with her, so it wouldn't be falling out of her hands.

She sat down at the kitchen table with a cup of coffee and went through it. One of the first things that caught her attention was a little envelope addressed to Rose.

"Rose, sweetie, you have mail."

She was in the living room playing with Snowball and Molly. Oops, Snowball just came running and hid in the laundry room, so it looked like she was done.

Rose walked into the kitchen, and Lisa handed her the envelope. It took her a while, but several rips and tears later, she pulled a card out of the envelope.

Lisa looked over her shoulder. "It's a birthday invitation to Megan's birthday. It says that Megan doesn't want any gifts but she requests that everyone bake cookies for the local soup kitchen along with some to pass out. It's a tea party."

Megan was already civic minded at age three?

"A tea party!" Rose just about swooned. "Can I wear my princess dress and sandals?"

"I don't see why not," Lisa said. "Oh, no! The party is this afternoon." She re-read the invitation. "It's in two hours. I have to bake cookies."

Lisa found a recipe for peanut butter cookies that looked easy enough. "Everyone stand back. This could get dangerous."

Rose giggled.

Lisa brought out a big bowl and began rounding up stuff for the cookies. She always thought that baking was like one big scavenger hunt. She'd never had everything she needed.

She thought she'd triple the recipe so she'd have enough. Doing the math in her head, she loaded up the mixer and turned it on.

It barely moved, and, after a while, she caught a whiff of hot motor oil.

"Maybe I ought to wait a while," she said to herself. "Let the machine cool."

She decided to pull some of the half-mixed dough out of the mixer. "I think I overloaded it, Rose."

Rose was sitting with Molly and Snowball and reading a book. She didn't care. She just wanted to go to the party and wear her princess outfit.

Lisa turned the mixer back on, but she forgot to take the spatula out. Dough splashed all over the kitchen. Lisa turned the mixer off and tried to pull the spatula out of the beaters.

"Oh, for heaven's sake." She took the beaters out of the machine and pulled on the spatula. It flew across the room and landed on the floor.

"I'm just going to mix this by hand. Like pizza dough," she said under her breath. "I've never made pizza dough, but I see them knead it all the time."

She did just that and was feeling good about the cookies. She pulled some dough off and made it into a ball, just like the instructions said.

She filled a cookie sheet and put it in the oven at 350 degrees. Then she filled another. The balls were perfect. She put that cookie sheet into the oven, too.

Making cookies was a snap. She snapped her fingers.

"The peanut butter cookies are in the oven, Rose. Easy-peasy."

Lisa cleaned the kitchen from the mess. She could have filled another cookie sheet from what was scattered around the kitchen.

Just then the doorbell rang.

Lisa wiped her hands on a towel and looked through the peephole.

Glen Randolph stood at the stoop with a slight scowl on his face as he peered at the chipped red pot of dried pansies sitting on her front porch that was desperate for a drink.

Lisa hoped the lawyer would see that she was a much better parent than a gardener.

She looked around the house and noticed how messy it was due to their recent trip, with clothes and storage bins stacked here and there.

The lawn looked like a hayfield. Sully hadn't had time to mow before he left. Lisa decided that she could do it, just after the cookies, and the laundry and taking Rose to the party.

Lisa plastered a smile on her face and opened the door. "Good afternoon, Mr. Randolph. Come in."

He walked into the house, and Lisa closed the door behind him. He shook her hand. "Hi, Lisa. How's everything going?"

"Great. Couldn't be better."

"I've tried to contact you for several days, and I even stopped by, but no one was home. I was getting worried. Until I watched the bull riding on TV and saw you, Rose and Sully there."

"We all went to Florida in Sully's motor home. I apologize. I should have called you."

He studied her. "Yes. You should have. Please let me know if you are going to be out of town again."

Oops. He was mad. "We will. I am really sorry, Mr. Randolph."

"Okay. It's forgotten, and call me Glen."

He turned to look at Rose. She was as cute as a bug on the couch with her book and her pets.

"I'd like to talk to Rose. Is that okay with you?"

Lisa held her hand out in Rose's direction. "Certainly."

He sat down next to her on the couch. "Rose, I'm Mr. Randolph. Remember me? I was a friend of your mommy and daddy."

"I miss my mommy and daddy." She held her hand out to pet Snowball, who had obviously decided to venture out of the laundry room where she'd been hiding.

"I know you do, honey, but Uncle Sully and Aunt Lisa are here for you. Are you doing okay?"

She shrugged. "I saw Uncle Sully ride a bull. He won. And I met lots of princesses, and I rode the rides and went swimming and lots of stuff."

"Sounds like a great time."

She looked up at Lisa, who was sitting in a chair opposite the couch. "Aunt Lisa, you have stuff in your hair."

Lisa felt her hair. It was loaded with cookie batter. "Excuse me. I'll be right back."

"Lisa, before you go, would you mind telling Sully that I'd like to speak to him, too?" Glen said.

She swallowed. For some reason, she didn't want to tell Glen Randolph that he wasn't here, that he was in Connecticut.

Rose answered for her. "Uncle Sully is bull riding. We're

going to have popcorn and watch him on TV. I hope he wins. He got hurt, you know."

Lisa scooted into the bathroom. She had a glob of batter on top of her head and another chunk dripping down the right side. She really should wash her hair, but for now she took a washcloth and got the worst off.

She could hear Rose talking to the lawyer about how she liked the trip, how she liked the motor home, how she liked to swim, how she liked the rides and finally how she was looking forward to the tea party this afternoon.

The cookies!

She raced into the kitchen and grabbed two potholders.

"Lisa, is something burning?" Glen asked.

"Seems like it."

Tentatively, she opened the oven door. Burned. Every cookie was burned, and the perfect little balls all ran together like lumpy charcoal.

Her beautiful trays of peanut butter cookies were a flat, burned mess.

"I—I just wanted to bake cookies for Rose's party. They were so beautiful and then...then..." She had more batter. Maybe she could pull this off, after all.

"It's my fault. I distracted you." He walked into the kitchen and surveyed the mess. "I'm an amateur baker. To me, it looks like your dough is too runny," he proclaimed. "Just add more flour and return it to the mixer."

"I think I burned out the mixer. I made three batches at once."

"Try it anyway, a little at a time."

The mixer must have healed itself. It was fine. Glen told her to add flour, then some sugar and a dollop of peanut butter.

"Rose, do you want to help me?" Lisa asked, wanting to involve her in the process.

"Okay."

As the two of them rolled balls, Lisa felt like every move she made was being scrutinized by the lawyer. Eventually, his smile and laughter at Rose's antics made her relax.

"I think your problem is that you're not measuring the flour correctly. I'll show you later."

"Thanks, Glen."

Lisa vowed to take a baking class, just after she took a cooking class.

"And you can't forget that they are in the oven," Glen said. "The recipe says ten to twelve minutes. Maybe a timer would help you remember."

"I'll put one on my shopping list." Lisa put her hand on Rose's shoulder. "Sweetie, why don't you read a book to Molly and Snowball?"

Rose went back to her position on the couch. Molly followed. Snowball was already on the couch, curled up into a ball.

"Sully should really be here doing this with you and Rose. It'd be a good bonding situation," Glen said.

"He really hated to leave, but we talked about him keeping his job and riding the circuit on the weekends. We mutually decided that it'd be okay that he rides, and I'm going to fly charters in the summer when he's on break."

Mr. Randolph rubbed his chin.

"Did we need to clear our employment with you? You know we have jobs."

"No. I was just thinking. It's a good compromise."

"Sully and I both realize that we all need to bond as a family. I think we have a strong start. The trip we just took in close quarters, in Sully's motor home, was a shortcut to bonding." She smiled. "Rest assured, Glen, that we are doing fine."

"Excellent." He checked his watch. "It's time to take the cookies out of the oven."

With potholders in hand, and holding her breath, she opened the oven. "They are magnificent! And they really look like cookies!"

"Can I see?" Rose came running.

Lisa took the cookies out of the oven and lowered them so Rose could see. "Careful, they're hot." She put them on the stove. "This deserves a celebration. How about some cookies and milk?"

She checked the fridge. "Oops, no milk. How about cookies and apple juice?"

"Sounds good," Glen said.

As they sat around the kitchen table eating her first-ever batch of cookies, Lisa couldn't help but wish that Sully was with them. He added something special with his personality, humor and devil-may-care attitude.

Lisa couldn't believe how much she missed him being around, and he had barely been gone one day.

Chapter Fourteen

When Lisa picked up Rose from the birthday party, her pretty princess dress was covered in mud, her hair was a mess, her face was dirty and she had a big smile—and blue frosting—on her face.

She had to say goodbye to all of her new friends before she got into the car. If Sully could see Rose now, he'd know Lisa was right about nursery school.

Rose chattered up a storm about the games they'd played, the kites they'd flown, and how they'd danced and had a sing-along.

Sounded like a fabulous time.

After giving Rose a bubble bath, Lisa put her down for a nap. Then Lisa went back to the mountain of laundry. For dinner, she was going to try and make baked chicken. She just needed to put some spices on it and stick it in the oven in a pan.

She could even toss some potatoes into the pan and boil some green beans.

How hard could it be?

The chicken was pink, the potatoes were too hard and the beans were soggy. Other than that, dinner came out great.

Lisa microwaved the chicken and potatoes and salvaged the meal. After coloring with Rose, playing dolls and watching the same cartoons for the ten millionth time, they finally sat down with a big bowl of popcorn and grape juice to watch the Professional Bull Riders on TV.

Rose wasn't much interested until Sully rode.

After being at an event in person, Lisa remembered the smells, the noise and the crowd. She could hear the clang of the gate as Sully's bull bounded out of the chute.

"Go, Sully!" she screamed. "Stay on! You can do it!"

"Ride, Uncle Sully!

"Six…seven…eight seconds! He did it, Rose! He did it! Yee-haw!"

"Yee-haw!"

Sully won the first round. Tomorrow, he'd ride again for the second round, then the final round.

When he was interviewed, he talked about the bull that he rode. Then he asked the interviewer if he could say hello to someone.

"Of course," the interviewer said.

"I'd like to say hello to Rose. She's very special to me." Then he blew her a kiss.

Rose giggled like crazy.

"And a big hello to Lisa, for many reasons."

He tweaked the brim of his hat, and Lisa melted. Why was he always doing sweet things like that?

Darn him!

The interviewer tipped her head coyly. "Who are these special ladies, Sully?"

He smiled his most charming smile and avoided the question. "They are very special to me, and I'd like to thank my sponsors…"

Lisa laughed. He sure had a way of changing the subject.

A big hello to Lisa, for many reasons.

What were those reasons? She'd love to hear them.

Darn him! He kept doing and saying nice things. This wasn't the Sully she knew: the drinker, the partier, the man without a care in the world.

Since they'd been thrown together, she'd found that he didn't drink or party, that he could discipline Rose when needed and that he could compromise with her when necessary. He made them both laugh and, as much as she hated to admit it, he was good for her, too.

But why was she still expecting that he was going to turn back into the Sully that she knew before? The Sully who cared for nothing but having a good time?

Shaking off the thoughts, she realized how late it was. "Time for bed, Rose."

Lisa tucked Rose into bed, and she listened to the girl's nightly prayers. "I want to pray for Mommy and Daddy and Aunt Lisa and Uncle Sully and Snowball and Molly. Amen."

She kissed her good-night, tucked her in and handed the Princess Mary Ann doll to her. Molly and Snowball got into position.

Back in the laundry room, she took a load of dry clothes out of the dryer and put another load in. Then she reloaded the washer.

Sitting at the kitchen table, she began to fold the dry clothes.

Her cell phone rang, and she looked at the caller ID. Sully. Her heart started beating faster, and suddenly her mouth went dry. She waited awhile before she answered to get herself together.

"Hello, Sully."

"Hi. How's everything going at home?"

"I had a surprise visit from Glen Randolph, Carol and Rick's lawyer and our inspector general."

"Did we pass?"

"He didn't particularly like the fact that you weren't here helping Rose and me bake cookies."

"So I can put out the blaze?"

"So we can bond like a family."

"Oh. You and I...we talked about that."

"I know. I told him that we discussed your traveling, and we have a plan that we both agree on. He liked that, but he didn't like that we left town without him knowing. He was making visits here to no avail."

"We'll have to remember to let him know. So, how's Rose?"

"Of course she misses you, but she couldn't wait to see you on television. I'll probably get the Bad Mommy Award from Glen Randolph for letting Rose stay up late and eat popcorn, complete with butter and salt."

"That's going to put you in the Bad Mommy Hall of Fame."

Lisa laughed. "In my defense, we did drink grape juice instead of soda, so this mommy might get a reprieve."

There was silence on Sully's end, then he said, "Do you realize that you called yourself *mommy?*"

"I did, didn't I?" Wow, that was a shocker. "You know, Sully, sometimes I do feel like I'm Rose's mom. I mean, I know Carol is her *real* mom, but I'm taking care of her the absolute best I can, and I've always loved her, maybe even more now."

"That's the definition of mother, Lisa."

A warm feeling came over her, like someone wrapped her in a fluffy blanket. Sometimes Sully knew just the right thing to say.

"Congratulations on your win, Sully. I'll keep my fingers crossed that you win tomorrow's event. That'd be two in a row for you. That'll kick you up higher in the rankings."

"Yeah. If I win tomorrow, I figure that I'll be third in the standings."

"Fabulous. How's the ankle?" she asked.

"It's still sore, bruised and swollen, but it's getting better. I can get it in and out of a boot at least. Don't worry about me."

I do worry about you. You're my partner in this.

They talked for more than an hour about anything and everything. They laughed, became serious and laughed some more.

Lisa couldn't remember when she had had such an enjoyable and intelligent conversation with a man. That the man was Sully completely baffled her.

"Tell Rose that I'll call her tomorrow," Sully said. "And I'll be home late Sunday night. We're driving home right after the event."

"Okay. See you then. Oh, wait! Sully?"

"Yeah?"

"Rose loved your shout out to her, and…um…I liked what you said to me. You said, 'And a big hello to Lisa, for many reasons.'"

"I remember."

"What are those reasons, Sully?"

"I'll tell you later. Remind me."

Her cheeks heated. They couldn't be that important if she had to remind him, for heaven's sake. Forget it!

Thank goodness he wasn't here to witness her embarrassment. "Good night, Sully. Be careful."

"Good night, Lisa. Sleep tight."

She couldn't sleep. She tossed and turned, thinking about Sully and how life had thrown her a curve ball, but she'd hit the ball and was running the bases as fast as she could.

And it seemed like she was running right toward Sully.

Sully had two back-to-back event wins under his belt. That was exciting, but he was even more excited to get home. However, he figured that he'd have to hit the road again soon. It'd take him a good four days to drive by himself to Anaheim, California, from Salmon Falls, New York. Then it'd be three days at the bull riding, then four days back for a grand total of eleven days. Or he could just drive straight to the next event in Indianapolis, from California.

He'd probably be gone for more than two weeks, if he detoured to Indianapolis.

He didn't want to spend that much time away from Rose and Lisa.

What could he do? He could find another bull rider to share the driving with, but that wouldn't trim off much time.

He swallowed hard.

Dammit. He had to fly.

Lisa waited up for Sully. For the most part, she read, but she kept looking for headlights coming down the road or up the driveway.

Earlier during the day, she and Rose went to the farm and tractor store—yes, the farm and tractor store—where her neighbor told her that she could find jeans. She'd bought two pairs of jeans and a couple of tops. There was even a pair of funky cowboy boots with flowers on them that fit her perfectly and were half-price. She had to buy them.

They even had cute sundresses and pajamas for Rose. Sold.

For Sully's return home, she slipped into jeans, one of

the striped T-shirts and her cute boots. She fussed with her hair and makeup a little more than usual.

What was wrong with her?

Finally, after midnight a car came up the driveway. Sully got out of the passenger's side and pulled his gear bag from the backseat. He went around to the driver's side and shook his friend's hand, gave him a wave and off he drove.

She watched as Sully stood and looked at the house. She couldn't see his face for his reaction, but she assumed that he was glad to be home, as he had alluded to in their conversation.

He slung his bag over his shoulder and strode up the brick walkway to the front door. Before he put his key in, Lisa opened the door.

"Welcome home," Lisa said.

Dropping his bag, he wrapped his arms around her waist, picked her up and twirled her in a circle.

Then he lowered her to the ground slowly, down the length of his body.

"Hello, Lisa."

"Hello, Sully." Her voice sounded breathy and low, probably because she was still stunned at his greeting and was trying to catch her breath.

She wasn't prepared for the big kiss that he landed on her.

His hand tangled in her hair and he rubbed her neck. She stared into his blue eyes, either waiting for him to make the next move or wondering why she couldn't move away.

"Now's the time to tell me to stop."

"But you haven't even started." She laughed, willing him to keep his fingers moving on her neck and praying that her knees wouldn't buckle.

He chuckled. "You're right. I haven't even started with what I'd like to do with you."

As much as she hated to spoil the moment, the front door

was open, the whole neighborhood could see them and bugs were flying in.

"Sully, the door is open—uh…neighbors and bugs."

Still holding her, he kicked out sideways, and the door slammed behind him.

"Any other objections?" he asked.

"Yes. Probably several. But I can't think of them right now."

"Good. Now stop talking."

His mouth touched hers, cautiously, carefully. She sighed at the pure pleasure, but she wanted more. She wrapped her arms around his shoulders, pulling him tighter. He kissed her harder, harder still.

She tugged at his jacket, not wanting anything between their bodies. He shrugged out of it and tossed it on an arm chair.

He stepped back, holding her hands in his. His eyes traveled the length of her body once, twice…

"You look great, Lisa. Like a real cowgirl."

She rolled her eyes. "Comfort. I was going for comfort, not cowgirl."

"That's why you bought those boots? Comfort?"

She shrugged. "I liked them. A lot."

"And I like *you,* Lisa. A lot. I've missed you." He hugged her close.

Being in his arms was pure heaven. She ran her hands over his back, feeling the bunching and constricting of his muscles. She had to touch his chest before she went crazy. Slowly, she pulled the snaps of his pale blue cowboy shirt, revealing a smooth chest with tight pecs and an even tighter stomach. She didn't neglect his chest, all soft and warm, yet tight and strong.

Sully was sheer perfection.

He tugged at her shirt, and she helped him remove it. Soon, it flew over toward the chair, missed and hit the floor.

Sully's lips traced a path from her shoulder to the vee of her lacy pink bra, and she couldn't breathe.

"Now's the time to tell me to stop, Lisa."

"Don't stop." It had been a long time since she felt so desired, so sexy. It was Sully making her feel this way.

Her bra hit the chair. Then her feet left the floor. Sully had picked her up as if she weighed no more than one of his gold belt buckles.

"My room or yours?"

She could barely think, but she knew that his room was farther away from Rose's. "Yours."

She tucked her head into his neck and inhaled his scent, a mix of leather and spice. She wanted him.

He gently set her on his bed and covered her with his body. The touch of skin on skin and his lips on hers set off something inside Lisa that had been dormant for a long time.

Along with their boots, the rest of their clothes hit the floor. She wanted to kiss every square inch of Sully, and when he pulled her on top of him, she got her wish.

He moaned in pleasure as her lips traveled lower and lower.

Sully was erect and hard, thick and perfect. She wrapped her hand around him, and he gasped. His hand covered hers. "You better stop, or this is going to be over too soon."

In one swift motion she found herself under him, his hardness pressing against her.

"Lisa?" Sully whispered.

She answered his question with a kiss. He traced her lips with his tongue and she opened for him.

"Make love to me, Sully."

"Damn!"

She chuckled. "Such charming love talk. You really know how to turn on a woman."

"Condom. In my wallet. Pocket of my jeans. On the floor."

"Damn!" she said.

With a grunt, he moved off her. She felt so…naked and cold without him. She concentrated on watching Sully, which wasn't hard. He was magnificent to look at.

"Got it." He pulled open the foil packet with his teeth and pulled out the condom.

"Let me do it." She moved to the side of the bed, and he handed it to her.

Slowly, she unrolled the flesh-colored disk over the length of him with one hand, holding him with the other. Sully's breathing became uneven, and when she was finished, he moved her back to the bed.

Leaning over her, he said, "That was the most erotic experience…"

His mouth played with hers, then traveled to her breasts. While his mouth teased one nipple, his hand teased the other.

She couldn't take it anymore. She guided him to her, and when he entered her, she gasped. He filled her slowly, allowing her to accommodate him. She was glad that he hadn't moved yet but just held her in his arms.

"Oh, Sully." She felt weepy, but that was crazy. She was just…happy.

He began to move his hips. Slowly at first, then faster. She met each thrust, giving in to her need for him.

"Lisa." He breathed her name over and over.

He slowed, then stopped, gathering her in his arms. He was prolonging their pleasure.

No!

She moved her hips, faster, faster still. She took him

deep, and when he shuddered, so did she, letting the waves of pleasure wash over her, feeling his heart pounding, enjoying his lips on hers.

They held each other for a while until he moved off her. Grinning, he planted a chaste kiss on her forehead.

She did the same to him.

She fell asleep with Sully hugging her close.

Sully woke up early. Six o'clock, according to the little clock on the nightstand. Sleeping next to him was Lisa, who he used to call the Ice Queen.

She didn't act like an Ice Queen last night—or should he say this morning?

She sure had melted.

He looked at Lisa. Her blond hair was a mess, her makeup was smudged and she was softly snoring. Yet she was the most beautiful woman he'd ever seen.

He shrugged into his jeans and headed for the bathroom. Looking in the mirror, he noticed that his eyes were red-rimmed and puffy, and he certainly needed a shave. He needed some long, uninterrupted sleep, but he wouldn't have changed this morning for anything.

Lisa Phillips? He'd made love with Lisa Phillips.

When he saw her last night, he couldn't help himself. Maybe it was coming home to a real house, a real woman and a little girl.

If he closed his eyes, he could imagine that it was all his, that Lisa and Rose were his family.

Damn. They *were* his family!

He hoped that things weren't going to change drastically between them. He'd given Lisa plenty of opportunities to stop things, but she hadn't. She was a willing partner—a very sensual one.

Going back into the bedroom, he put a hand on her shoulder and shook her gently.

"Hmm?"

"Lisa?" he whispered in her ear. "I think you'd better move to your bedroom."

Her eyes shot open. "Huh? What?"

She wasn't a morning person.

"You're in my room. You might want to scoot to your room before Rose wakes up."

"Yeah." She looked under the sheet, obviously saw that she was naked and grunted. She put her hands over her face, rubbing her cheeks. He couldn't read her reaction.

He put his hand on her waist. "Regrets?" he guessed.

She turned and smiled at him. "Uh…um…of course not."

That didn't sound too convincing.

Wrapping the sheet around herself, she got up, scooped up her clothes from the floor and padded down the hall.

He could hear her bedroom door shut.

In the cold light of day, he could tell that Lisa Phillips had regrets.

And that made him feel like a fool.

Regrets?

Lisa was unsure how to answer that, so she blurted out something so as not to hurt Sully's feelings. It was too early in the morning to think, and she hadn't had any coffee.

She slipped into the shower and let the warm water sluice over her. She ached in places that she didn't know she had.

From the second he came into the house last night she couldn't keep her hands off him.

Sully had been a sensitive and caring lover, and he admitted that he "liked" her. That was the only compliment that she'd received from a man in a couple of years. It had been a long draught without sex.

Was she attracted to Sully simply because he was here? Or was it more than that?

Chapter Fifteen

Lisa slipped on jeans and a T-shirt and joined Sully in the kitchen. She felt as if she had a hangover, while he looked bright-eyed and cheery. Lucky him.

Rose walked into the room, wiping the sleep from her eyes. When she saw Sully, she broke out in a big smile and took off at a run to him. He scooped her up and lifted her over his head.

"How's my little princess?"

"I'm good."

He lowered her to the ground. "Do you have a kiss for me, Princess Rose?"

"Uh-huh."

He pointed to his cheek, and she gave him a sweet kiss where he indicated. Then he pointed to his other cheek. Another kiss. Then his forehead. Kiss. He did that several more times and was rewarded each time by a giggling Rose.

Sully sure could make them both laugh.

Lisa wished she had his spontaneity, but she was getting there. Just yesterday, didn't she buy those funky cowboy boots? Didn't she let Rose stay up past her bedtime to see Sully ride? Didn't she just register for cooking classes?

Her class, cleverly titled "Really Basic Cooking for Microwavers Anonymous," would start in September, just when Rose would be eligible to attend nursery school.

Her cooking class was scheduled for three mornings per week. She wouldn't even need a babysitter.

Lisa hadn't forgotten that Sully promised to visit the nursery school. She should arrange that soon—maybe now while he was around.

While Lisa had cereal and Rose had oatmeal on the patio in the backyard, Sully tried to fire up the lawn mower.

Yeah, right.

He'd never seen such a temperamental engine in his life.

He was going to repair it or die trying. He'd fixed it once, and he was going to fix it again.

Finally, he got it to turn over—to the applause of the breakfast club on the patio.

Lisa held up a mug of coffee as a toast to him, or maybe she was offering him a cup. He climbed up onto the mower, put it in gear and drove it to the patio. As he bucked by on the mower, which was about to stall, he smoothly snatched the coffee cup from Lisa's outstretched hand and mowed a wavy line on the backyard grass.

Rose put her hand over her milk-covered face and giggled. Lisa cupped her mouth with her hands and shouted, "Hey, Sully. Rick and Carol's lawn probably never had to suffer a mowing pattern like that!"

He liked the squiggly pattern. It was different.

As he mowed, he thought about how he had made love with Lisa last night. He'd thought about it when he was in the shower, when he was scarfing down some toast with peanut butter, when he was working on the lawn mower and now.

She was always on his mind.

He looked at her sitting at the table. She was chatting away with Rose. That was one of the things he liked about her, how she talked to Rose. Lisa didn't talk down to the little girl or use that singsong voice that mothers often do. Above all, Lisa listened to the little girl.

He'd even noticed that Lisa was loosening up. She'd probably never be the spur-of-the-moment type, but she was acting more relaxed in the situation that was thrust upon both of them.

Sully wondered if things would continue to be comfortable between them. He didn't want to tiptoe around her just in case she made a big deal out of their making love.

He didn't think it was a big deal. They were both consenting adults, mutually attracted, so they acted on their attraction.

Normally, Sully would make love to a woman, and he'd be gone in a couple of days. Very few women did he call and make an effort to see again. As a matter of fact, he could count them on three fingers.

With Lisa, he really couldn't pack up and leave. They were living under the same roof. They'd had a rocky history, and they faced an uncertain future. All he knew was that the present was pretty good between them.

He never thought he'd say it, but he liked the mammoth Victorian. He even liked this Podunk town.

Which reminded him—he was going to ask Lisa if she'd like to accompany Rose and him on their "walk around" sometime today. Maybe they could have lunch at his favorite diner, and he could get a haircut. They could take Molly for a walk and go to the playground, too.

Yep, Brett Sullivan, the third-ranked bull rider in the

world right now, hadn't been interested in sticking around after the Connecticut event to party with the guys and the buckle bunnies until the wee hours of the morning.

Instead, he couldn't wait to get home.

And now he was looking forward to a walk with his ladies to downtown Salmon Falls, just after he finished putting the last touches on his brother's...no, *his*...brilliantly green lawn.

Life was good.

Lisa could hear the faint ringing of her cell phone inside the house, and she got up to answer it.

"Stay right here, Rose. Watch Molly and keep an eye on Uncle Sully so he doesn't fall off."

"Okay."

She missed the phone call but waited until the caller could leave a message. Then she dialed the code for her voice mail.

"Lisa, this is Luann from JFW Aviation. I know this is short notice, but I really need you. I have a charter this weekend to Anaheim, California, that I need you to fly. Departure is Friday. Return is on Sunday. The man who booked the charter said that no one but you can pilot the plane. He's very persuasive. Charming, actually. I think you'll enjoy this one. Call me immediately so I can confirm with him."

Lisa listened to Luann's message three times.

Wasn't Sully headed for Anaheim this weekend?

For a nanosecond Lisa wondered if Sully might be the one who was booking the charter, but she quickly dismissed the thought because he was so mulish about not flying.

Besides, a charter from Albany to Anaheim, round-trip, would cost in the neighborhood of fifty-five thousand dollars.

Sully had that kind of money. He'd told her that he was a millionaire, but apparently he didn't spend his money.

Would he spend that kind of money on a weekend?

Lisa could picture herself in the cockpit of a super mid-size, something like the Citation X. She could see the instruments, somewhat different than the wide-bodies. She could feel the vibration of the tires as she taxied. Then came takeoff—her favorite part of flying—when all the mighty thrust of the jet engines finally got the plane off the runway and into the air.

She didn't know why she was dreaming about it. She couldn't take the charter. Sully was off to Anaheim himself, and she needed to take care of Rose.

Her daydreams would have to wait awhile longer.

She picked up the phone to call Luann back when she was distracted by a scream.

Rose's scream.

Sully jumped off the tractor and ran toward Rose. Lisa came running out of the back of the house onto the patio. The screen door hit the side of the house with a loud bang and stayed open.

He could see Rose was running along the side of the house, heading for the front yard and the traffic on the street.

"Rose, stop!" Sully yelled, but she'd had a head start.

Lisa ran next to him. "What?"

"Molly's chasing a squirrel. Rose is chasing Molly."

"Sully, she's heading for the street!"

"Will she stop?" Sully asked.

"I don't know!"

Why did the yard have to be so big?

They both raced after Rose. She was almost to the sidewalk. Sully caught up with her first and picked her up under his arm like a football.

He handed her off to Lisa.

"You know you shouldn't go past the sidewalk and into the street, don't you, Rose?" Sully asked.

"Molly! I want Molly!"

She couldn't care less about the rules.

Molly, however, had crossed the street and was running like her fur was on fire. Rose was sobbing on Lisa's jeans.

"I'll catch her," Sully said. He gave a sharp whistle, but it didn't stop Molly. The dog was several houses down on the neighbor's lawn.

He could hear Rose sobbing and calling the dog's name. He heard Lisa tell her not to worry because Uncle Sully would find Molly.

His bum foot was throbbing, but he tried to ignore it. Thank goodness he was wearing sneakers instead of his cowboy boots so he could run faster.

Molly disappeared, so he stopped to catch his breath. When he did, he gave another sharp whistle. "Molly," he yelled. "Come!"

Despite spending time with Molly at the house and in his motor home, he really didn't know how well the dog was trained, but he vowed to start training her to at least come when she was called.

He began to jog, then picked up his pace. He spotted the black dog stretched out like a caterpillar.

When Sully caught up with Molly, he collapsed next to the dog and joined her in breathing heavily.

"Molly, Lisa is crying for you."

Her ears twitched.

"Let's go back." Sully stood and Molly did the same. Sully took his belt off and slid it through Molly's collar for a quick leash. "Sorry, pal, but you just lost your free-range privilege."

Lisa and Rose were walking down the sidewalk to meet them. When Rose saw him with Molly, her face lit up. She said something to Lisa, who dropped her hand, then Rose started running up the sidewalk.

Sully had a death grip on Molly's leash. They were too close to the road to trust the dog.

Rose caught up with them and immediately hugged the stuffing out of Molly. "Thank you, Uncle Sully, for bringing Molly back."

"Don't forget to thank your aunt Lisa. She helped, too."

By then, Lisa had arrived and Rose thanked her.

He noticed how pale and zombielike Lisa looked. "Thanks, Sully," she said, her lips barely moving.

He handed Rose the makeshift leash and told her to stay close. He took Lisa's hand, and they followed Rose down the sidewalk.

"You look like you are in shock," Sully said. "Do I need to throw a bucket of cold water on you?"

"Probably," she said. "I'll never forget Rose's scream. It robbed me of ten years of my life. I thought that something had happened to her."

"I could hear her scream over the noise of the mower. That had to be a lot of decibels! She can really hit the high notes."

"I could use a drink right now."

"What do we have in the house?" he asked.

"Apple juice and lime Kool-Aid. The apple juice is Rose's, the green Kool-Aid is mine. And it's strong stuff."

He chuckled and squeezed her hand. "I'll pour us both a stiff one when we get back."

"Shaken, not stirred," Lisa said.

Sully laughed, then he realized that walking hand in hand with Lisa, joking while Rose walked ahead with the dog, was so...domestic.

When they came closer to the Victorian with his motor home parked out front, he felt warm and fuzzy.

Fuzzy?

Brett Sullivan, the rolling stone, wanted to stop rolling. He wanted to mow the damn huge lawn. He wanted to weed the garden, plant tomatoes, watch things grow.

Watch Rose grow.

"Sully, just for grins, I have to ask you something."

"Hit me with it."

"Did you by any chance charter a flight to Anaheim this weekend with JFW Aviation and request me as pilot?"

"I did."

"Why the hell didn't you tell me?" She pulled her hand out of his and slipped it in the pocket of her jeans.

"I was going to tell you. I wanted to tell you over lunch at the diner during our walk around."

"What diner? What walk around?"

"I didn't get a chance to ask you about going on a walk around, either. To the Salmon Falls Diner in town—you, me and Rose."

"But you don't fly," she said, getting back to the subject.

"I have to fly. I can't stay away from home that long for three reasons. One, I don't want to. Two, I'd like to think that you and Rose want me here. Three, Lawyer Randolph might think I'm interrupting our family bonding too much."

"All good reasons," Lisa said. "But it'll cost you a fortune! And what about your fear of flying?"

"I figure you can get me through it."

She raised an eyebrow. "Sully, I'll be flying the plane!"

"Oh, yeah. Good point." They walked on the side of the house to the backyard. "We're bringing Rose with us. Rose can help me."

Lisa froze. "How can she help?"

"I'll refrain from crying like a baby so as not to scare her."

Lisa shook her head and grinned. "I see you have this all thought out...not!"

"We can discuss it over drinks on the veranda." He slipped into his finest British accent, which he didn't think was all that bad. "Let me serve you ladies. And I shall prepare a bowl of fine water from the garden hose for the wayward canine."

"Sounds divine," Lisa said.

"Coming right up."

After drinks on the veranda, as Sully had said, they freshened up and walked to downtown Salmon Falls. Lisa loved the historic buildings and the way the variety of goods, services, crafts and restaurants with their different storefronts all blended in.

It was a thriving place compared with other small towns. Nothing was boarded up and there were no gaudy banners or signs, just a cute, tasteful town full of fountains, statues of war heroes, gazebos, trees and colorful flowers.

"You know, Sully, being here in downtown Salmon Falls always makes me wish that I had experienced small-town life. I'd have a bunch of friends from school that I could ride bikes on the sidewalk with. We'd get an ice cream cone, go to the movies and hang out on the benches in the town square. Maybe there'd be a band playing in the gazebo we could listen to. I would have gone to that beautiful library over there and would have read a book on that bench over there." She pointed to the library with its three-story pillars and a bench by a copse of Canadian hemlocks. "Instead I lived in a commune in the middle of a field. No wonder Carol and Rick wanted Rose to grow up here."

"I've traveled all over the United States on the circuits, and I have to agree with you. Salmon Falls has it all." He steered Lisa to the park bench she'd pointed to.

Rose found a boy about her age, and they were swinging on the swings together, so they had some time to talk.

"You know, Lisa, this isn't the first time you've brought up the commune. There must be some good things about it that you liked."

"I'll try to think of some positive things," she said, then shook her head. "Nope. Nothing."

"Come on. Think."

"I got closer to my sister, Carol, although Carol loved commune life as much as I hated it."

"What else?"

"I liked being outside all day long."

"Good."

"And I liked one particular teacher. I looked forward to him coming up in the rotation," she said. "Sorry, Sully. That's about it."

"The experience made you what you are today."

"Yes. And now this experience will enrich my life even more." This time, she took Sully's hand. "I can't believe everything that's happened to us in such a short time."

"No kidding. Who would have thought?" He pulled her up from the park bench as Rose approached. "Would you ladies like to accompany me to Joe's Barbershop?"

"Uh, no. We'll sit here on the bench," Lisa said. "Go. Get handsome for when you take us to the diner. We don't go out with just any third-ranked bull rider." She turned to Rose. "Right?"

"Right!"

Lisa had an interesting conversation with Rose about bugs (some bite, some just crawl), what she'd like for lunch (pancakes and French fries), how her daddy took her to the hardware store (and it stunk like paint) and how her mother always took her to the store over there (where she got her princess dress and sparkly sandals).

Finally, Sully walked down the sidewalk in their direction. He overexaggerated a swagger, and Lisa laughed so hard she couldn't catch her breath. Rose jumped up and imitated him.

Lisa hesitated. She couldn't, could she?

She jumped up from the bench, and the three of them did the Sully swagger all the way to the diner.

Sully liked it when Lisa loosened up. He would never have pictured the Ice Queen doing anything silly like she just had. Never.

He had to stop thinking of her by that nickname. Again, he thought of last night, this morning, whatever time they had made love. He wondered what she'd do if he came into her room tonight. Would she throw him out or welcome him?

He held the door of the diner open for them. The line of red stools at a low counter, the strong smell of coffee and grease and the booths lining the wall all screamed diner and comfort food.

As they slipped into a booth, Rose immediately started playing with the buttons on the breadbox-size jukebox hanging from the wall.

Sully handed her two quarters, and his niece figured out how it worked without much coaching from them.

After the first few notes, he and Lisa both identified the song as "Blue Moon." They sang along a bit as Rose stared at them. Then the waitress dropped off menus and rattled off the specials.

The three of them talked and laughed until she came back to take their order.

She stared at Sully. "Hey, aren't you Brett Sullivan, the bull rider?"

"Guilty as charged," Sully said.

"I watch you on TV. Can I have your autograph?"

"Sure."

She pulled up her royal-blue Salmon Falls Diner T-shirt to expose her midriff. Lisa raised an eyebrow. Rose just stared.

The waitress handed Sully a felt marker. "Write 'I love you, Shannon,' then sign it."

"I won't do that. I don't sign body parts, and I don't say I love you to very many women. As a matter of fact, I've never said it."

He took the placemat full of colorful advertising, turned it over and signed his name, along with "Bull Riders Rule!" Then he dated it and put "Salmon Falls, NY," under that.

"Well, that's cool, too." She took the placemat. "I'll be back for your order."

After she'd left, Sully rolled his eyes.

"Have you signed a lot of body parts, Sully?" Lisa whispered as Rose returned to punching buttons on the jukebox.

"You can't believe what women want signed and what they want me to say. I'm up for fun like the next guy, but I have to draw the line somewhere."

"That was pretty classy of you not signing her...um... stomach," Lisa said.

Her approval meant a lot to him.

She leaned over the table and said softly, "Did you mean the part about how you've never said 'I love you' to a woman?"

He looked deep into her emerald eyes. She wasn't mocking him—she was serious. "I've never said it to anyone I've been with. Not yet, anyway."

Lisa looked thoughtful. "I've never said it to any man I've dated, either. None of them has ever mattered that much to me."

"Maybe someday..." Sully said.

"Yes. Maybe someday."

Chapter Sixteen

Lisa helped Sully buckle Rose and Princess Mary Ann into one of the eight bucket seats of the Citation X. She'd told Luann that she wanted the Citation X for the large fuel tank, and it had been available.

Sully buckled himself into the divan across from Rose. A table was between them for playing games or snacking. Both seats were right behind the cockpit.

Lisa didn't know what she could do if Sully had a meltdown other than to make him put on an oxygen mask and breathe.

She had a portable one ready.

"Rose, you and Uncle Sully can play games, and he can put together a puzzle with you. I can even put on a movie if you'd like."

"Um…" She looked up at Lisa. "Do you have the fairy movie?"

"Oops. Sorry," Lisa said. "I should have brought yours from home, but I forgot."

"That's okay."

Disappointment showed on her cute little face, and Lisa felt terrible. How could she have forgotten Rose's favorite movie?

"I'll play with Uncle Sully," Rose said, brightening.

Sully was staring down at his seat belt. "I'm not feeling that great."

"Breathe," Lisa said. "This cabin is about as big as the inside of your motor home. Pretend you're there."

"My motor home doesn't fly," Sully mumbled.

Rose tilted her head. "Are you sick, Uncle Sully?"

"Rosie, sweetie, I've never been in an airplane before."

"Me, either," she said. "Do you want me to hold your hand?"

Lisa bit her lip so as not to laugh. Here was a three-year-old trying to help a big, tough bull rider.

The irony wasn't lost on Sully. "I'd love for you to hold my hand."

"We'll be traveling at about six hundred miles an hour, so we'll be in Anaheim in a little more than four hours," she said. "You can hang in there for four hours, Sully."

"Six hundred...what? Why did you have to tell me that?" he said, gripping the arms of the beige leather divan.

"I thought you knew how jets work, cowboy. They go fast," Lisa said, trying unsuccessfully not to laugh.

"You'll be okay, Uncle Sully."

"And if you're not, there's a full lavatory in the back." Lisa pointed to the rear of the aircraft, then put her hand on the portable oxygen tank. "And if you're queasy, put this on."

Lisa took one last look at her niece's little hand slipped into Sully's big, calloused one.

How she remembered his hands from the other night!

Lisa raised her fist in a cheer. "Let's get going to Anaheim. Right, passengers?"

"Right!" Rose shouted.

"And let's hear from my other passenger. Sully? Hey, Sully? Bueller?" She mimicked the famous movie.

"Right. Let's go," he mumbled, glaring at her.

Lisa hurried to the cockpit and settled in. She got the okay from the tower to taxi to the runway.

Her heart started to pound as it always did when she got the go-ahead to move. It wouldn't calm down until she was at cruising altitude.

This was the most important flight of her life because of her passengers.

As she waited on the runway, she said a prayer and ended it by saying, "A safe flight, dear God. A safe flight for the two most important people in my life."

Sitting there, waiting, it hit Lisa that they—all three of them—were a family.

Sully couldn't believe that he was sitting in this flying burrito about to go six hundred miles per hour. The one thing preventing him from telling Lisa to turn around was sitting across from him.

He didn't want Rose to think of him as a whimpering, simpering coward, which he totally was right now.

He knew that the burrito was about to move—and fast. He knew that he might let out a scream that would break the sound barrier before the Citation X would.

As he hyperventilated, he knew he had done the right thing by taking Rose along for this short weekend. Glen Randolph told him so. Randolph was also impressed that he chartered a plane and Lisa would be flying it.

But Randolph didn't know that on takeoff, Sully was

about to pull the upholstery off the little couch he was sitting on.

He heard Lisa's voice over the loudspeaker. He could barely hear her over his heavy breathing.

"Rose, Sully, sit tight. We are cleared for takeoff. This is going to be fun, Rose. Just like a ride at an amusement park."

This is hardly a ride, Sully thought. *More like a nightmare.*

He heard the roar of the engines, and he held his breath. He knew he could hold it for eight seconds, but now he was going for the record. He'd hold it until they landed in California.

Rose rocked in her seat. She thought this was a great adventure.

She was young, he told himself. She didn't know about the law of gravity yet.

Rose reached over the table and offered her hand, and his heart melted. "It's okay, Uncle Sully," she said sweetly.

It was difficult, but he pried his right hand off the seat and held hers.

They took off from the runway, and he heard a loud "yee-haw" from the cockpit.

He concentrated on not squeezing Rose's hand too hard.

Finally, they leveled off, the loud noise quieted somewhat, and he could breathe if he wanted to. He debated it.

Rose looked out the window. "Can we see our house?" she asked.

Sully immediately picked up on the fact that she called the big Victorian "*our* house." Maybe Rose was accepting Lisa and him as her parents, or at least as her guardians.

He turned toward the cockpit. Lisa amazed him in that she knew all about those little dials and levers and whatnot around her and even over her head. She was one smart woman.

He forced himself to look outside. The sky was blue and there were several fluffy white clouds.

"The clouds look good enough to eat, don't they, Rose? They look like cotton candy."

Rose picked up Princess Mary Ann and pressed her against the window. "See, Princess?"

Sully relaxed. Okay, maybe this plane thing wasn't so bad. Actually, it was like sitting in a chair. He could hardly tell that they were moving unless he looked out the window. Even looking outside wasn't that bad. It was kind of…nice.

"Lisa? Can I get up and stretch my legs?"

"Are you okay?"

"Surprisingly, yes."

"Bravo!"

Sully walked around the cabin, then checked out the bathroom. It was all stainless steel and pretty roomy. He checked out the galley, where there was a fridge stocked with sodas and juices. He took two cans of fruit punch for Rose and himself.

After a while, he sat back down.

Rose took a sip of her juice, but it dribbled down her pretty pink dress. Shoot! He should have looked for paper cups.

He went back to the galley and found some cups and some paper towels. Hurrying back, he pulled out some towels from the roll and dabbed at the front of her dress. The stain was still there.

Rose looked like she was about to cry. "This is my pretty pink dress that Aunt Lisa bought me."

"It's okay, Rose. Aunt Lisa will get the juice marks out and your dress will be as good as new. You'll see."

Suddenly, with tears dripping and out of the clear blue, Rose asked, "Are you and Aunt Lisa going to get married?"

"Why do you ask that?"

"Because I heard Grandma Sullivan say that it's wrong for you to live together without being married." She took another sip of juice, this time from the cup.

Leave it to his mother to say the most inappropriate thing at the most inappropriate time.

"Can I be a flower girl?"

Sully was at a loss as to how to answer her questions, but he might as well give it a go because the questions would only get harder as Rose got older.

He should really think of a good answer to this one that wouldn't leave Rose screwed up for life.

"Aunt Lisa and I have a special relationship. We are both taking care of you, so we have to be with you, together."

Sully was proud of himself with that answer.

"But are you going to get married to Aunt Lisa?" she asked.

She was too young. She didn't get it. He was just about to say no when he thought about it.

Married to Lisa?

He could imagine being married to her. They laughed together. They had Rose in common, bull riding and the big house on twenty acres.

He grinned. The sex was great, too.

They both liked RVing, and chili, and theme parks, and jeans, and cowboy boots, and now—believe it or not—Sully was enjoying flying.

Some marriages were built on less.

Lisa had been pretty amazing during this arrangement.

She wasn't a cook—that was for sure. She could master flying any size plane, but she couldn't master the oven. Forget the stove top.

But she tried. She'd tried baking, too, and that didn't go very well, but she'd hung in there and, with a little help, made cookies for Rose's party.

If he thought of what he liked the most about Lisa, it would have to be her willingness to compromise. Their job situation was an ongoing problem, and Lisa could have really screwed him with his PBR weekends, but she hadn't.

And he paid her back by swallowing his fear and chartering this plane so she could fly.

"You go, Lisa!" he shouted. "Crank this machine up to six hundred and *one* miles an hour!"

He grinned and leaned back on the divan, feeling smug.

"Rose, if your aunt Lisa and I ever get married, you can be the flower girl."

"Seat belts on. We're going to land soon," Lisa said. "Rose, are you ready?"

"Ready!"

"Sully, are you ready?"

"Ready!"

"Then let's land this bird!"

Lisa liked landing almost as much as takeoff. She loved the thump of the tires as she released them. The reversing of the engines, the squeal of the brakes...it was all a thrill.

She taxied to her assigned gate. "We're almost here. Stay seated, guys."

Sully surprised her. He was a head case before, but he had soon relaxed and enjoyed the flight.

They arrived at the gate, and the hustle began with the ground crew. She had to do some paperwork, so she asked Sully and Rose to wait for her somewhere. Rose wanted some chocolate milk, so Sully pointed to a restaurant in the terminal called On the Fly.

"They probably have chocolate milk," Sully said. "We'll meet you there."

Lisa breezed through the red tape and caught up with them at the restaurant.

Rose's face was covered in ketchup. She was dunking her French fries in it and seemed to be missing her face. She had more ketchup on her dress, along with chocolate milk and juice stains.

Lisa didn't know if she had the laundry skills to save the dress, but she'd give it a try.

They didn't have to stop at the luggage pickup, so Sully hailed a taxi to their hotel.

After a long, slow ride due to the traffic, they finally arrived at their hotel.

Sully had reserved a suite with two rooms and a kitchenette. Lisa thought that was a brilliant idea because they would all be able to stay together. The suite was airy and well-lit and had a beautiful view of palm trees and the pool with a lazy river and waterfalls.

Sully came up behind her and they both looked out the window. He was so close that she could feel his breath on her neck when he spoke.

"There's a nice area for kids. Rose will love it."

She wanted Sully to slip his hand around her waist and pull her to him, but with Rose nearby, he'd never do that.

But Sully was always full of surprises. He did slip his hand around her waist and pulled her closer to him. In silence, they watched the action at the pool.

Sully whispered in her ear, and delicious shivers ran up and down her spine.

"We can work in a little recreation while we're here, but let's each swear that we won't tell Rose that California has a bunch of theme parks and water parks," Sully said.

"I swear," Lisa said with definite enthusiasm.

"Shall we hit the pool?" Sully said.

"I'll help Rose change into her suit."

Fifteen minutes later, they were ready for the pool. Sully found lounge chairs in the kiddie pool area right in front of

Rose, who was content chasing squirts of water that popped up randomly around her.

Sully and Lisa stretched out on the lounge chairs near misters. She liked the fact that if she looked at misters in a certain way, she could see rainbows.

Lisa looked around at the palm trees and the cascading flowers and ferns. She felt like she was in the middle of a tropical island—a tropical island with a couple hundred adults and four hundred kids, give or take.

"This is heaven, Sully."

"Sure is," he said. "If I closed my eyes, I could almost imagine being stranded on a tropical island."

"I was just thinking the same thing!" Lisa snapped her fingers. "Sully, if you were stranded on a tropical island and could only take three things, what would they be?"

"My lasso. As you know, I sort things out as I rope."

"I know that, but you haven't roped in a long time, so things must be okay. What's number two?"

"Probably a new RV." He waved to Rose, and she waved back. Then she went back to the squirting water. "I've been thinking of getting a new one."

"I don't get it. Aren't you going to be flying now that you're cured?" she asked. "Flying commercial, I mean. It's way cheaper."

"I still want to drive whenever I can. I like the parking lots at events, like the potluck meals, and I like to hang out with everyone."

"I did, too," she said, and she meant it. She'd met several people who she'd love to see again. They were probably here, so she'd make a point to look them up. "Okay, Sully, what's the third thing you'd want on a deserted island?"

"You."

The telltale warmth immediately hit her cheeks and started spreading like a pink stain. Her mouth went dry.

"Whew, that was a surprise," she said. "Tell me why."

"Because we're good together. I'm not just talking about sex—I'm talking about several things."

The waiter arrived with their drinks then. She'd ordered a virgin strawberry margarita, And Sully had ordered a beer.

Lisa couldn't wait to get back to their conversation, although the mood was broken.

Sully held up his beer for a toast. "To Lisa, who I'd love to have with me on a deserted island because we have intelligent conversations, we compromise, we have heated discussions that I enjoy and I think we make a good team—Team Rose. Life wouldn't be dull on that island if you were there."

She smiled. She liked his "several things." "Thanks, Sully."

He leaned over and was about to kiss her on the cheek, but she turned her face so his kiss would land on her lips.

"I wish I could peel that bathing suit off you and make love to you right in the middle of that waterfall over there." He pointed to the one on the left. "I'll meet you here tonight around midnight after the bull riding."

Her cheeks couldn't get any hotter or her mouth any drier. She sipped her drink.

"What about Rose? We can't leave her alone."

"I have it covered," Sully said. "I called a friend of mine. She'll watch over Rose. Rose will be sleeping anyway."

"I can see you have everything all planned. What if I don't show?"

"I think you will."

"You're pretty sure of yourself, aren't you, cowboy?"

"Sure am." He winked and tweaked the brim of his cowboy hat. Then he stood and pulled his bathing suit away from his crotch.

They made eye contact and smiled.

"I'm going to take Rose on the lazy river. Hopefully, it'll be cold water."

Lisa grinned. It made her feel sexy that she could turn him on.

"Then I have to get ready and head to the arena," he said. "Would you like to join us in the water?"

"I think I'll stay here and enjoy my drink."

"We'll meet you back here."

As she watched him take Rose's hand and walk through the crowd, Lisa thought about Sully's proposition. It excited her and made her apprehensive at the same time.

But what happened to her position that they should be just friends?

Their first encounter was simply to get rid of the tension. They gave in, it was fabulous and that should have been it.

If things didn't work out between them, could they go back to being friends and living under the same roof until Rose was eighteen?

Fifteen years was a long time.

They were adults, she decided. They could work things out for Rose's sake.

Lisa knew one thing for sure—she'd be waiting under that waterfall at midnight and would deal with the consequences later.

Chapter Seventeen

Sully bribed the security guards to let them through the locked gates and into the pool area.

It was worth the two hundred bucks.

Only a few lights were on, giving the place a surreal look. It was a beautiful evening, warm with a slight breeze. It was a perfect night to make love with a beautiful woman.

He was glad that Lisa had met him. He had come right from the fan club signing after the event. Earlier, Lisa and Rose had ridden back to the hotel with his friend Barbara Brennan, who worked in the Pueblo, Colorado, office of the Professional Bull Riders. She was going to watch Rose for a while.

When Lisa slipped off her dress, a type of cover-up, he couldn't believe his eyes. She wore the hottest red bikini with silver beading on it.

Wow.

He took her hand and they walked down the steps into the pool, then over to the waterfall.

The rush of the falls over the rocks, the noise when it hit the standing water and the spray made it seem like they were in their own little world.

As the water sluiced over them, Sully couldn't stop kissing Lisa. She seemed like she was enjoying the moment, too. Her arms were around his neck, and her legs were around his waist.

She had to feel his erection through the thin fabric of her bathing suit.

She stood, bent over and then tossed her suit bottoms on one of the rocks. Sully did the same with his trunks. Then he picked her up again. But this time he slid into her and she gasped. He stroked her hard and fast, and she met him move for move.

He knew he was going too fast, and he slowed down for her to catch up with him.

When he started to move again, Lisa threw her head back. He kissed her neck, her jaw, her lips.

"Faster," she said.

He obliged.

He heard Lisa whisper his name, and she closed her eyes and groaned.

Waves of pleasure washed over him as he let himself go, holding on to Lisa as if she were his lifeline.

Sully walked Barbara out to the lobby, where the bellman whistled for a taxi for her. He went back to the hotel room and joined Lisa in the shower.

After toweling off, they adjourned to Sully's room and made love again.

Later, they spooned together and Sully had never felt so content.

"Are you happy, Lisa?"

"Mmm…I am, Sully. I really am."

"Have you had any thoughts about us getting married?"

"Married? Us?" He could feel her tense. "I haven't given it much thought—if any. No. No. Not at all."

He thought she protested too much, or she definitely was repulsed at the idea of marrying him.

"We can't get married, Sully. We shouldn't. There's too much to consider. There's too much at risk."

"Like what?"

"What if we didn't make it and got divorced? How do we share Rose? You'd be the weekend daddy, and I'd be the primary care mommy? Oh wait…you work and travel on weekends. We'd have to reverse those roles. I wouldn't want Rose to have to go through a divorce after losing her parents."

"So you don't think we can go the distance?" Sully asked.

"I don't know. We're so different."

"We have a lot of things in common."

"Superficial things."

"They're not so superficial, Lisa."

"It'll be too complicated. Can't we just go on like we are?" she asked.

He grunted. She was just making excuses.

"Yeah, we can go on like we are," he said.

He felt mad and then stupid. He'd thought she'd feel the same way he did about them getting married.

"I know!" He snapped his fingers. "We can raise Rose during the day and sneak into bed the second she takes a nap in the afternoon or goes to sleep at night. We could always have a sitter on standby in case we have an immediate urge for sex. Maybe we should have two sitters on standby. Let's synchronize our watches. Ready, set, sex!"

Lisa moved away from him. She didn't say a word but

pulled the sheet off the bed, wrapped it around herself and walked out of his room.

Sully felt like all his happiness was draining from his body. He didn't realize he'd fallen so hard for Lisa.

He loved her, dammit!

But she obviously didn't feel the same way about him.

What the hell was that about?

Lisa slipped into her nightgown and stood in the middle of her bedroom in astonishment.

Sully and she had just made love a couple of times, and they were perfectly content and sated. Then Sully asked out of the freaking blue how she felt about marriage.

What kind of a question was that? Was he asking her to marry him or to think about marrying him? Besides, he never even told her that he loved her. What was he doing—testing the waters?

Or did he think that their marriage would make Rose more secure or make his parents happy? His parents were old-school. Her hippie parents couldn't care less.

She'd told Sully her reasons why they should remain status quo, but he dismissed them without much consideration.

As she slipped into bed, she decided that she should have told Sully the truth—that she had wondered several times what it would be like to be married to him. That's how she came up with the reasons it wouldn't work.

Then again…maybe it would work. Maybe they should take the chance.

Aw, hell! She might as well admit that she loved him! Yes, she wanted to marry him. Maybe on some occasion he'd even ask her nicely, but only if he loved her back.

Three days later, Sully stood in Carol's garden, roping the statue of Athena yet again. He'd been there forever tossing his lasso, going to the statue, pulling off the loop and roping it again.

He must have something on his mind.

So he roped Athena.

After Lisa drained a glass of iced tea, she decided that the garden needed weeding, so she yanked out things that she hoped were weeds and not flowers. She got to the sign that said "Carol's Garden. Fairies enter here." She'd always think of it at Carol's garden and vowed to keep it blooming in memory of her.

Lisa sat down at the concrete bench to take a break. Sully looked over, wound his rope and walked over to join her. She made room for him, knowing that he had something to discuss with her.

He grinned. "I have a birthday present for you."

"My birthday isn't until next week."

"I know, but I wanted to give you this early so we can plan. We're going to need babysitters."

He pulled a card out of his jacket pocket and handed it to her.

Intrigued, she opened it. "Dancing lessons!"

"Ballroom dancing lessons. Didn't you tell me once that it was your dream to take ballroom dancing lessons?"

"You remembered!"

"Of course I remembered." He extended his hand to her. "But first things first."

He got down on one knee.

"Sully, what on Earth? Oh my…"

"Lisa Phillips, I admire you. I love talking to you. We have yin and yang." He smiled. "I love how we are raising Rose together, and I'd love to raise even more children with you, if we are so blessed. I love you, and I'd be honored if you'd marry me. We can adopt Rose and really make her ours."

"Yes, yes, yes! I'll marry you, Sully. I love you. I really do." She looked up at all the windows of the big Victorian. "I want to fill those rooms."

He pulled a ring out of the pocket of his jeans. "This was my grandmother's. I'd like you to have it but, of course, if you'd like another ring, we could go to the jewelry store and I'll buy whatever you like, and—"

"I'd love to wear your grandmother's ring!"

Sully slipped it on her finger. It fit perfectly.

She helped him up, and they kissed. It was a special kiss because it was in Carol's garden, and it sealed their promise of love.

Lisa knew that they'd always compromise and work together. She knew that there would always be laughter in the big, old Victorian thanks to Sully, although she could hold her own with him now.

Sully knew that there'd never be a dull moment with Lisa. She was one special and smart lady. Besides, she liked his motor home.

To make the moment even more perfect, Rose burst out of the house, ran right to them and hugged them both.

"I saw you, Uncle Sully! I saw you kneel down and ask her. And then you kissed Aunt Lisa a really long time!"

Sully laughed. "Your aunt Lisa said yes. We're going to get married, Rose."

She turned toward Lisa. "Aunt Lisa, am I going to be a flower girl?"

"You sure are, sweetie!"

"Yee-haw."

It was Sunday. Yesterday they had all flown commercial to Indianapolis for three days of bull riding. Today, the bull riding was at two o'clock. They had time to have a nice breakfast buffet and to attend Cowboy Church in the arena before the event.

Sully left to get ready for the event, and she and Rose took a walk around the event center. They stopped for cotton candy, and Lisa made Rose sit down to eat.

What a mess! They had to spend a half hour in the ladies' room getting the cotton candy out of Rose's hair and off her face and fingers.

Lisa heard the arena come to life, so they hurried to their assigned seats. The riders were introduced, the national anthem was played and the bull riding was set to go.

Sully was going to be the last to ride because he'd won yesterday's event. It was a long wait for Sully, and Rose was very fidgety in her seat and getting cranky and tired. She just wanted Uncle Sully to ride, and there was nothing Lisa could do to get her to calm down.

Lisa asked Rose to sit on her lap, and Lisa rocked her to sleep. The tired little girl just needed an afternoon nap.

Finally, it was Sully's turn. Lisa debated whether to wake up Rose, but in the end she decided to let her sleep. She'd probably get a hash mark against her name in the Bad Mommy Hall of Fame, next to the hash mark for "forgot Rose's special DVD to watch on the plane."

Sully drew a very rank bull, Bullistic, who had never been ridden and who had been out more than forty times. The arena announcers were in awe of Bullistic, calling him "the meanest bull on four hooves."

The gate opened and Bullistic jumped in the air as if he were in Swan Lake. He twisted and turned, and Sully went flying, but not before he smashed his face on the bull's horns. Sully lay on his back on the arena dirt, out cold.

As the bullfighters tried to keep Bullistic away from Sully and get the bull back behind the chutes, Sully lay unprotected in the arena. The sports medicine team couldn't get to him while a bull was loose.

Bullistic spotted Sully and took off after him. He rolled him several feet with his horns. Sully looked like a rag doll being tossed around. He was still out cold, his face was bloody, and Lisa thought that he'd lost some teeth.

Lisa held her breath. She was about to scream, but she didn't want to wake Rose. She was thankful for her decision not to wake her for Sully's ride. Seeing Sully hurt and bloody would upset their niece.

Just when the bull was about to go into the gate, he made another charge at Sully. He threw him in the air with his horns, and Sully landed yet again on the dirt.

Finally, Bullistic was roped and back behind the chutes.

The sports medicine team rushed out. The lead doctor examined Sully as a hush fell over the arena. Sully wasn't able to answer any questions presented to him.

They strapped him onto a board and carried her fiancé out of the arena.

The announcers said that they were rushing Sully to an area hospital and that he was still unconscious.

Lisa needed to know which hospital Sully was being taken to. She'd take a taxi there.

Lisa woke up Rose and they both left their seats. Lisa tried to get to the back where the contestants were, but she was stopped. Then Security took one look at the tears running down her face, her drippy nose and a sleepy girl in tow, and they rushed her to Sully's ambulance.

Barbara Brennan appeared, thrust a wad of tissues into Lisa's hand and offered to take Rose back to the hotel room and watch her.

Lisa could have cried harder for the kindness. Instead, she blotted her face, blew her nose and squatted to her niece's level.

"Rose, Uncle Sully got hurt riding his bull. He's going to the hospital to see a doctor. Will you go to the hotel with Mrs. Brennan while I go to the hospital with Uncle Sully?"

"I wanna go with you!" She started to cry. "I wanna see Uncle Sully."

The ambulance attendants were motioning for Lisa to get into the ambulance.

"Please, Rose. Do what I ask. You'll see Uncle Sully soon enough, but not now, sweetie. Go with Mrs. Brennan."

"No!" she screamed.

"Just go, Lisa," Barbara said. "She'll be okay."

What could she do? She had to go with Sully.

In spite of Rose's screams of anguish, Lisa hurried to the ambulance.

Once she was in the ambulance and Rose's screams were replaced by the howl of the siren, Lisa looked at Sully. She couldn't see much because he was been attended to by the EMTs, but what she did see brought a fresh bout of tears to her eyes.

She looked down at her engagement ring. It sparkled when the ambulance lights hit it just right.

"Sully, wake up. Please, wake up and be okay," she whispered. Then she prayed.

Sully tried to smile at Lisa when he first woke up in the emergency room. She wanted to hold his hand, but she didn't dare—he was so broken and bloody.

"You should see the other guy." Sully could barely talk, and she could barely understand him. He had an IV with three bags dripping into him and gauze in his mouth and towels under his chin to sop up the blood from his missing teeth.

"Sully, how can you joke at a time like this? You were almost killed."

"It goes with the job."

"Time for another job, don't you think? You have a daughter...I mean, you have Rose to think of."

"She *is* our daughter. She really is...our daughter."

Whatever was in the IV bags was lulling Sully to sleep.

Lisa leaned over and kissed him on the forehead. Then she whispered in his ear. "Yes, she is our daughter, and we're a family."

They were just about ready to take Sully to the operating room. They told Lisa that she could accompany them as they wheeled him down the hall.

Just as he was about to enter the O.R., she kissed him on the forehead again—the only spot where he wasn't battered—and whispered in his ear, "I love you, Sully. Get better, hear? I can't do this alone."

And then she prayed some more...and let her tears fall.

"I just saw the surgeon—three to be exact. My bull riding career is over," Sully said quietly, evenly. "No Vegas for me this year or any other year. There go all my plans. If I'm not a bull rider, what am I?"

Lisa had never seen Sully so down. After five days in the hospital, he was ready for discharge. He would still need a lot of follow-up care in Albany and Syracuse, but he was deemed fit to fly home tomorrow.

"Bull riding is what you do, but it does not make you who you are, Sully. You're a father to Rose. You're my friend and partner in raising her. You're a mentor to a lot of young bull riders. You are kind to the kids who adore you. You are many things."

He turned his head away. "By the way, you were right, Lisa. You were right when you said that there's no future for us. So, let's just remain friends and get marriage right off the table. We wouldn't want Rose to pick up on any discord or animosity between us."

"That was before, Sully. I was wrong. I wasn't willing to take a chance on us. I guess I was just…scared. But all that has changed, Sully. We're going to get married. Remember? You got down on one knee and asked me. You gave me a ring to seal the deal."

He studied her. "Everything has changed, Lisa. Don't you get it? All my money will probably go into paying for all this."

"I'm not marrying you for your money. I have enough for the both of us." Lisa's heart sank, and she felt sick to her stomach. "Forget about money, for heaven's sake. We love each other. We are partners. We can work through this."

"You won't love me for long after you have to do everything. I'm going to need foot surgery and spinal surgery, so I'm going to be in a wheelchair for a long time, and I can't drive, and then there's rehab and then—"

"We'll do it all. Together. That's what people who love each other do."

"I've never had to depend on anyone. That's not me."

"So change."

He turned away.

"Look, Sully. You're going to walk again, so count your blessings. Some others aren't as lucky as you. And you'll be there for Rose because you won't be straying farther than Carol's garden in the back of the Victorian for a while!"

Sully didn't smile.

"That was a joke, Sully. A joke!"

He sighed. "You might as well know that I've been thinking of calling Glen Randolph and telling him that I'll turn over Rose's guardianship to you. You'll make a better parent, anyway."

"Dammit, Sully. Haven't you heard anything I've said?"

Lisa felt the blood rush to her head in anger. She tried counting to ten, but she only made it to three.

"The surgeon must have removed your heart instead of your spleen, and your brain must be broken instead of your ribs and your cheekbone. Or maybe it's the morphine talking, but we are a pair, cowboy. Remember, yin and yang? So snap out of your funk before we fly out of here tomorrow. Rose hasn't seen you in a week, and I don't want her to be scared…or disappointed."

Tears came to her eyes, and she turned to leave before Sully saw them.

"Lisa?"

She didn't move. "What?"

"Find someone else to love. I'm not worth it."

She took a deep breath, slid her beautiful ring off her finger and handed it to him. "Give this back to me when you stop feeling sorry for yourself and realize what you're losing—Rose and me. Besides, we promised Rose that she'd be a flower girl at our wedding, and we don't want to let her down. And someone gave me the gift of ballroom dancing lessons, and I'm holding him to it."

Sully didn't want to scare Rose, so he put his cowboy hat over the bandages on his head. The bandages covered a row of thirty stitches and a strip of scalp where they'd had to shave his head.

He'd lost a couple of teeth, and his mouth was damn sore, so he barely moved his lips when he talked.

There was more, but he had to wait to get home to start rehab and have a couple of operations.

Home. Funny how "home" was the Victorian, not his motor home.

He looked at Lisa's engagement ring, which he wore on his pinkie finger. After the stupidity he spewed yesterday, it would serve him right if Lisa left his butt on the curb instead of picking him up at the hospital in a taxi. He realized what a dope he'd been, especially after a group of his fellow bull riders stopped in to see him.

They kicked his butt even more than Lisa, and she'd done a very thorough job.

She was right. He'd walk again, and others weren't that lucky. He'd been reminded of that when Jerry DiNardo had rolled in with his wheelchair. Jerry had been thrown by a bull some twenty years ago and had been confined to a wheelchair since. Yet Jerry worked his ranch, went to rehab every day and volunteered for every new treatment that came his way with the hope that he'd walk again.

Jerry had married a special woman and adopted a bunch of kids. He said that he was the happiest man alive, and there was no reason for him to feel sorry for himself.

Sully felt like a petty jerk and vowed that he'd have the shortest rehab possible. He'd work like a rented mule and show Lisa that he didn't mean what he'd said. It was just a momentary lapse in good sense when he realized that all his goals had crashed and burned around him.

Then he realized that only his bull riding plans had to be changed. His personal life was like a dream come true. He still had Lisa and a daughter he loved.

He had a lot of explaining and apologizing to do. Fingers crossed that Lisa would accept his apology.

There was a slight knock on the door, and Lisa entered his room.

"Just answer one question," she said, barely stepping into his room. "Have you snapped out of your funk, or do Rose and I leave for the airport without you?"

He sat up straighter in his wheelchair and removed his hat. "Can you ever forgive me for...for being such a jerk?"

"I downgraded you to B-movie actor for your lack of

acting ability." She smiled slightly. "So, what's the plan? If you are running away in your motor home, maybe I should point out that you are unable to drive. Or are we going back to being a three-person family living in Salmon Falls?"

"I like the Victorian, but I really *love* the two ladies who live there with me."

He held out his hand to Lisa and held his breath that she'd take it.

She did.

He kissed the back of her hand and then pulled her toward him, giving her ample time to resist.

She didn't.

She kissed him ever so gently on the side of his mouth, due to the stitches on his upper lip. He wanted so much more and made a mental note to get to the dentist first, so his mouth would be in better kissing shape.

"Will you marry me again?" He held up her engagement ring and held his breath.

"I thought you'd never ask, again." She held out her hand and he slipped it on her finger. Then he kissed the back of her hand.

When he looked up, there were tears swimming in her eyes.

"Aw…why are you crying, Lisa?"

"I'm happy. Can't you tell?"

He grinned. "I guess I'll have to get used to it."

Lisa slipped her hand from his as a nurse appeared with a wheelchair for Sully. "Rose can't wait to see you."

"Where is she?" Sully asked.

"Downstairs in the taxi with Barbara."

"What if I had decided not to come home?"

"I knew you'd come to your senses. You're a tough bull rider, Brett Sullivan, and you're not a quitter. I gave it a lot of thought and I think you might have been offering me a way out of our engagement, although I don't know why you thought so little of me to conclude that I wouldn't stick around to help you and would just walk away."

"You're not a quitter, either. I should have known."

Lisa shook her head. "I just think you'd just forgotten about the traditional 'in sickness and in health' part of the marriage vow. It's the health part that's the easiest."

Sully slid his hat onto his head. "Then it's good that we're going to get the hard part over with first."

Epilogue

"It was a beautiful wedding, Lisa. I especially enjoyed it when you and Brett danced together. Why, it almost seemed that you two had been taking lessons!" Sully's mother smiled as she flipped through pictures in a photo album. "And I am so sorry for doubting you and Brett."

The other grandparents nodded.

Lisa chuckled and took Sully's hand. "We had the same doubts."

Rose skipped into the dining room, wearing her princess/ bridesmaid dress yet again. Lisa had to beg her to take it off so she could wash it from time to time.

"Aunt Lisa flew our new plane to Loz…Loz…"

"Las Vegas," Sully supplied.

"Las Vegas. Right, Uncle Sully?"

"That's right, sweetie."

Lisa smiled. With Sully's new contract as a PBR announcer, they'd decided that they'd all travel together on the weekends as much as possible, and that meant that they'd all flown together to Las Vegas for the PBR Finals.

Lisa and Sully had gotten married on the grounds of the South Point Hotel and Casino after the Finals were over. All the parents had flown in for the wedding, which had been packed with bull riders, stock contractors, pilots and flight attendants.

Today, though, the celebration was in Rose's honor. Lisa lit the pink candles on the child's pink birthday cake.

"Blow out the candles, Rose!" Lisa clapped.

"One-two-three-four! I'm four years old now."

"You're getting to be such a big girl," Sully said, snapping pictures.

The grandparents grinned. They had flown in for Rose's birthday celebration, her nursery school play and, most importantly, her official adoption in family court by Sully and Lisa, which would take place tomorrow.

Sully and Lisa had explained at length to Rose that they would like to make her their "official" daughter, if she'd like that. She agreed as long as her mommy and daddy would still watch over her in heaven.

"You really made those chicken tenders, Lisa?" her mother asked.

"And they were even edible," her father added.

"Yes, I did. They're Rose's favorite. And I made the baked potatoes and the salad. I even made the dressing. I bought the cake, though."

Sully put his arm around her and squeezed. "Lisa has graduated to Cooking 201 now."

"Amazing," said Lisa's mother. "I never would have believed that Lisa would actually cook."

"And that Sully would stop riding bulls," Sully's father added.

Lisa and Sully exchanged a knowing look. If their parents

only knew the ups and downs they'd experienced, mostly due to Sully's accident... But it made them even stronger.

But Lisa didn't want any of that kind of talk around Rose, so she hurriedly cut the cake and passed it around so they all could concentrate on eating.

"Rose, why don't you sing the song about the flowers and frogs to your grandparents while I talk to Uncle Sully for a moment? Okay?"

"Okeydokey!"

Lisa took Sully's hand and they walked over to Carol's garden. Sully had a slight limp, but the doctors felt that as more time passed, even that would disappear. They took a seat on the bench.

"It's time to finally open Carol and Rick's letter, Sully. It's the day before we go to adopt Rose. It's the right time."

He put his arm around her shoulder. "Are you sure you can handle it?"

"Yes."

She pulled the letter out of the envelope, took a deep breath, then read:

If you're reading this, then we aren't here in the physical world.

You might be wondering why Rick and I decided to appoint you both as guardians for Rose. It's because we couldn't think of two more loving parents for our little girl (other than us, of course).

We know you can't stand each other (!), but we hope you'll put aside your differences to do what's best for Rose.

We always thought you two were perfect for each other. I can see you laughing now, but miracles do happen.

Raise our daughter as if she were yours. Love her and remember that we love you both immensely.
Kisses,
Carol and Rick
P.S. Lisa, take care of my garden, or I'll haunt you. C.

* * * * *

SPECIAL EXCERPT FROM

H HARLEQUIN®

SPECIAL EDITION

When a dangerous storm hits Rust Creek Falls, Montana, local rancher Collin Traub rides to the rescue of stranded schoolteacher Willa Christensen. One night might just change their entire lives....

***

"Hey." It was his turn to bump her shoulder with his. "What are friends for?"

She looked up and into his eyes, all earnest and hopeful suddenly. "We are, aren't we? Friends, I mean."

He wanted to kiss her. But he knew that would be a very bad idea. "You want to be my friend, Willa?" His voice sounded a little rough, a little too hungry.

But she didn't look away. "I do, yes. Very much."

That pinch in his chest got even tighter. It was a good feeling, really. In a scary sort of way. "Well, all right, then. Friends." He offered his hand. It seemed the thing to do.

Her lower lip quivered a little as she took it. Her palm was smooth and cool in his. He never wanted to let go. "You better watch it," she warned. "I'll start thinking that you're a really nice guy."

"I'm not." He kept catching himself staring at that mouth of hers. It looked so soft. Wide. Full. He said, "I'm wild and undisciplined. I have an attitude and I'll never settle down. Ask anyone. Ask my own mother. She'll give you an earful."

"Are you trying to scare me, Collin Traub? Because it's not working."

He took his hand back. Safer that way. "Never say I didn't warn you."

She gave him a look from the corner of her eye. "I'm onto you. You're a good guy."

"See? Now I've got you fooled."

"No, you don't. And I'm glad that we're friends. Just be straight with me and we'll get along fine."

"I am being straight." Well, more or less. He didn't really want to be her friend. Or at least, not *only* her friend. But sometimes a man never got what he wanted. He understood that, always had.

Sweet Willa Christensen was not for the likes of him....

***

Enjoy a sneak peek at USA TODAY *bestselling author Christine Rimmer's new Harlequin® Special Edition® story,* MAROONED WITH THE MAVERICK, *the first book in* MONTANA MAVERICKS: RUST CREEK COWBOYS, *a brand-new six-book continuity launching in July 2013!*

REQUEST YOUR FREE BOOKS!

2 FREE NOVELS PLUS 2 FREE GIFTS!

✦ HARLEQUIN®

SPECIAL EDITION

Life, Love & Family

HARLEQUIN

SPECIAL EDITION

Life, Love and Family

Be sure to check out the last book in this year's
Mercy Medical Montana miniseries by
award-winning author Teresa Southwick.

Architect Ellie Hart and building contractor
Alex McKnight have every intention of avoiding
personal entanglements while working together.
However, circumstances conspire to throw them
together and the result is a sizzling chemistry that
threatens to boil over!

Look for Ellie and Alex's story
next month from Harlequin® Special Edition®
wherever books and ebooks are sold!